SKULL MESA

Center Point
Large Print

Also by Wayne D. Overholser and available from
Center Point Large Print:

**This Large Print Book carries the
Seal of Approval of N.A.V.H.**

SKULL MESA

A WESTERN STORY

Wayne D. Overholser

CENTER POINT LARGE PRINT
THORNDIKE, MAINE

This Center Point Large Print edition
is published in the year 2019 by arrangement with
Golden West Literary Agency.

The text of this Large Print edition is unabridged.
In other aspects, this book may vary
from the original edition.
Printed in the United States of America
on permanent paper.
Set in 16-point Times New Roman type.

ISBN: 978-1-64358-239-9 (hardcover)
ISBN: 978-1-64358-243-6 (paperback)

Library of Congress Cataloging-in-Publication Data

Names: Overholser, Wayne D., 1906-1996, author.
Title: Skull Mesa : a western story / Wayne D. Overholser.
Description: Center Point Large Print edition. | Thorndike, Maine :
    Center Point Large Print, 2019.
Identifiers: LCCN 2019011385| ISBN 9781643582399
    (large print : hardcover acid-free paper) | ISBN 9781643582436
    (large print : softcover : acid-free paper)
Subjects: LCSH: Large type books. | GSAFD: Western stories.
Classification: LCC PS3529.V33 S58 2019 | DDC 813/.54—dc23
LC record available at https://lccn.loc.gov/2019011385

Chapter One

Clay Roland saw the horse and rider when they were so far out on the desert that they were cut down by distance to the size of a slowly moving dot. He stood in front of the Paiute City jail, the fall sun glinting on the silver-plated star on his vest, his gaze on the approaching horseman as he speculated about him. He might be a cowhand from a nearby ranch or he might be a stranger; he might be a friend or an enemy.

Six years' service as a lawman had taught Clay many things. The one that caused him the most concern was the fact that, when he pinned on the star, he made himself a target. Dead men had friends who were bound to catch up with him sooner or later, so, as a matter of habit, he gave every new man a careful appraisal.

When this one reached town, Clay saw that he was a complete stranger. At the moment he had no way of knowing whether the man was an enemy or a friend, so he remained on the street, wanting the rider to see his star. Often that was enough to determine whether a newcomer was hunting him or not.

When the stranger was opposite the jail, Clay saw that he was young, probably eighteen and certainly no more than twenty. He sat evenly balanced in the saddle as a good rider does who knows how to spare himself and his mount. Judging from the coat of dust on both the horse and the rider, they had come a long way since dawn.

Their eyes met briefly, then the stranger looked away and rode on as if to say his business in Paiute City had nothing to do with the law. Suddenly he seemed to realize he had come to the end of the trail. Probably he was anticipating a drink and supper, Clay thought, and perhaps a shave and bath and a good night's sleep as well.

The boy straightened in the saddle, alert now, his gaze swinging from one side of the street to the other. He was looking for somebody, Clay decided. It might mean trouble, it might not, but if it did, he would be involved whether the kid was looking for him or not.

Clay watched the boy turn into the livery stable. Presently he appeared in the archway and stopped, glancing up and down the street. Even at this distance Clay saw that the kid carried himself with a sort of arrogant certainty, his revolver holstered low on his right thigh and tied tightly in place as it would be with a man who realized that his life depended on the speed of his draw.

The boy stood there a full minute as if wanting to make sure he was seen, the afternoon sun throwing his long shadow against the boardwalk.

6

Then, slowly and deliberately, he turned toward Kelly's Bar and went in.

The kid's brand seemed easy enough to read. He had come to make trouble. If Clay was guessing right, he had the choice of going directly to the boy and facing him, or waiting it out until the kid made his move.

In a case like this, Clay was never sure which was the right choice. If he picked the first alternative and the kid was proddy, he might cause trouble that was unnecessary. On the other hand, if he waited, he might permit a killing that could be avoided. Better play it slow, he decided. There was always a possibility he had misjudged the kid. There was also the chance the boy had said something to the liveryman about his reason for stopping in Paiute City. The next town was twenty miles away, long miles across a red rock desert that was never a pleasant ride. Maybe the boy knew that, or had been told, and so was stopping for the night.

Clay strode past the saloon and went on into the livery stable, his thoughts turning sour. He should be thankful for trouble. It created a job for him. If there wasn't any, a town would have no need of a marshal. Still, it was a hell of a situation when he got jumpy every time a strange, gun-packing kid rode into town.

He thought about law officers he knew who had served twenty or thirty years and had stayed alive to save enough to buy a ranch and retire. He knew of others who had been killed the first year they had worn a star.

He turned into the gloom of the stable, thinking how often he had considered doing something else. He had a few hundred dollars saved, but not enough to buy a ranch or a business. And he didn't have a home to go to. His father wanted no part of a son who was a gunman, whether he was on the right side of the law or not.

"Pop!" Clay called.

The liveryman stepped out of a stall halfway back along the runway. "I was going after you if you didn't show up purty soon," the old man said. "The kid who just rode in was asking for you."

Clay drew his gun and checked it and slipped it back into leather, thinking he had known all the time that this was the way it would be. He knew something else that was even more disturbing, that regardless of how this particular affair came out, sooner or later he would meet a stranger who was faster than he was or who would wait for a chance to shoot him in the back.

Clay raised his gaze to the liveryman's face. "Did he say what he wanted me for?"

The old man shrugged. "No, but he's sure got the looks of a tough one. You see the way he carried his gun?"

"I saw it, all right," Clay said, "but it didn't

8

prove anything. You can wear a gun the right way and still be slow."

"I wouldn't count on it." The liveryman shrugged. "Hell, it's your business. I didn't tell him you was the marshal. I said if he waited in Kelly's Bar, you'd show up sooner or later. I got the notion he knowed your name and nothing else."

"Thanks, Pop," Clay said. "I'll see what he wants."

He turned toward the archway. Before he reached the boardwalk, two shots slammed into the afternoon quiet from Kelly's Bar, coming so close together that the second might have been an echo of the first. He ran toward the saloon, wondering how there could be trouble before the kid even found him.

He drew his gun as he rammed through the batwings. The boy lay on his face near the bar, his gun on the floor within inches of an outstretched hand. Except for the bartender, the big room was empty.

"Blacky Doane done it!" the bartender yelled. "Gunned him down, by God. The kid pulled his iron, but he wasn't fast enough."

Clay kneeled beside the boy and, lifting a wrist, felt for the pulse. There was none. He had been shot through the heart. Clay rose, asking: "How did it happen?"

"Nobody but me and Blacky Doane was here,"

the bartender said. "Doane was sitting at a table, playing solitaire like he's been doing ever since he rode into town. You know how he was. Never said a word. Tight-mouthed, Doane is."

Clay nodded, knowing exactly how it was with Doane. Ten days ago the man had ridden into town as much of a stranger as the dead boy. He had put his horse in the stable and had taken a room in the hotel, and since then had spent nearly every waking hour playing solitaire in Kelly's Bar. Not once had he indicated where he had come from or why he was here. Now it was plain enough he had been waiting for the boy, but how did Clay fit into the picture?

"Go on," Clay said.

"Well, this kid walks in like he was tougher'n a boot heel," the bartender continued. "Swaggering as if he wanted everybody to know he was the proddy kind. He comes up to the bar and asks for a beer. I give it to him and he bitches about it being warm. All the time Doane was watching. Purty soon the kid slams a letter down on the bar and says he's looking for you. He's supposed to deliver the letter to you personal. Says he'd been looking for you for a couple of weeks."

"What happened to the letter?" Clay asked.

"I'm getting to that," the bartender said. "When Doane hears that the kid has this letter for you, he gets up and says he'll take it. I guess the boy thought Doane was you till I told him different.

Then he says for Doane to go to hell and puts the letter in his pocket. Doane starts toward him, saying he'll take that letter if he has to blow the kid's head off to get it. Right then the kid goes for his gun, but Doane beats him to the draw. That's all there is to it. You've got nothing to hold Doane on. The boy drew first and that's a fact."

"The letter, damn it!" Clay shouted. "What happened to the letter?"

"Oh, the letter. Well, Doane kept his gun on me and told me to stand pat, then he kneels down beside the boy, takes the letter out of his pocket, and goes out through the back door in a hurry."

Swearing, Clay wheeled toward the door. Pushing through the crowd that had been attracted by the shooting, he left the saloon on the run. Doane must have been sent here to keep the boy from delivering the letter. Now that Doane had the letter, he'd try to get out of town fast.

Clay guessed right. Doane was in the livery stable saddling his horse when Clay got there. He said: "I want the letter, Doane."

The man stepped out of the stall into the runway. He faced Clay, his legs spread, right hand close to the butt of his gun. He said: "I didn't aim to make you no trouble, Marshal. I was paid to keep you from getting this letter. The kid would've been all right if he'd given it to me like I told him."

"You're making the trouble," Clay said. "For yourself if you don't give me that letter."

"I wasn't paid to kill you, Marshal," Doane said, as if trying to reason with a stubborn child. "They don't care whether you're dead or alive. They just don't want you coming back. Now I always do what I'm hired to do and I was hired to keep you from getting the letter, so don't push me."

"Who hired you?"

Doane hesitated, then said: "I don't know, Marshal, and that's the truth. Abe Lavine contracted me, but I don't know who got him to do it. I never asked. Fact is, I didn't want to know. Abe told me where you were. A man like him always has ways of knowing them things. The kid didn't. He had to hunt for you and that's why it took him longer to find you. Now I'm climbing into the saddle and I'm leaving town, so get out of my way and keep on living."

"You'll leave town when I get my letter," Clay said.

"Now look, Marshal," Doane said, "the letter ain't worth dying for. You sure ain't got no cause to hold me. Killing the boy was self-defense. He pulled first. If you make me kill you, I'll do it, but it ain't smart. It just ain't smart."

Doane might be the man who was faster than he was, Clay thought. There was no way of knowing until it was tested. Doane was right, too, about having no cause to hold him. Clay didn't even know how important the letter was, or what Doane had meant about someone not wanting him to go back. That could refer to any of a dozen places, to any of a dozen people. He knew nothing about Abe Lavine, either, except that the man was a notorious gunfighter.

The point was it had become a personal thing now. A boy had died trying to deliver a letter to him. If Clay had stopped him as he'd ridden past the jail and told him who he was, this wouldn't have happened. But what was past was past; all he could do was to play it out from here.

Clay let the seconds pile up, smiling a little at Doane. This was one of the tricks he had learned. He didn't feel like smiling, but it was a mark of confidence. Let the other fellow see you were dead sure, let his nerves tighten until he broke. Maybe Doane would, maybe not. You never knew.

"All right, Doane," Clay said softly. "I've given you plenty of time to think it over. You're the one who'll decide whether you'll die or not. If you don't want to, give me my letter."

He paced slowly along the runway toward Doane. Now uncertainty had its way with him and he broke as Clay hoped he would. He threw the letter into the litter on the barn floor. "To hell with it," he snarled, and, wheeling toward his horse, led him out of the stall and stepped into

13

the saddle. He dug in the steel and went out of the stable on the run, scattering the men who had gathered in the archway.

In one of the back stalls the liveryman let out a long sigh. He asked: "How'd you know he'd cave?"

"I didn't," Clay said curtly, and, picking up the letter, left the stable.

He returned to the jail, ignoring the curious stares of the townsmen who stood on the board-walk.

Chapter Two

Clay sat down in his office and threw the letter on the desk in front of him. The envelope was worn and dirty from being carried in the boy's pocket. Two words were written on it: *Clay Roland.* That was all. The handwriting seemed vaguely familiar, but Clay could not identify it.

He rolled and lit a cigarette, thinking that the letter had caused the death of the boy and had very nearly caused his or Doane's. He'd do well to throw it away and never look at it. The chances were it was an offer of a job from some other town where he had worked. Leadville. Trinidad. Santa Fe. Tucson. Hell, it could be any of a dozen places.

He picked up the envelope and started to tear it in two, then stopped. Some friend might be in trouble and was sending for him. Friend? He laughed silently. In six years of drifting from one tough town to another, he had formed no friendships. He had none here in Paiute City.

His life was as empty as a man's could be. That was one of the penalties he paid for being a lawman. You were always caught in a squeeze between the law-abiding and the lawless. If you killed a man, you were censured by one side; if you didn't, you were criticized by the other. If you were offered a bribe by the lawless ones, you were condemned by the righteous; if you turned it down, you were doubling the chances of being killed.

The worst of it was that when the chips were down, you could seldom count on the good people backing you. As far as friendships were concerned, it never paid to form any. Friends only added to a lawman's troubles. If they broke the law, they expected their friendship to get them out of trouble. So one thing was sure. The letter had not come from a friend.

He tore off the end of the envelope and drew out the single sheet of paper. If someone thought the letter was important enough to hire Blacky Doane to keep him from getting it, the least he could do was to read it. He unfolded the letter and sat up, suddenly alert. It was dated October 3rd, a little over two weeks ago, and was signed by Anton Cryder, a lawyer who was his father's best friend.

Quickly he read:

Dear Clay:
The last anyone in Painted Rock heard from you, you were in Santa Fe. I have no idea where you are now, so I cannot mail this letter to you. That's why I'm hiring Ernie Layton to find you and deliver the letter personally. He's just a boy and

sometimes he's a little smart-alecky, but he's about the only person on Skull Mesa I can trust. If he stays out of trouble, he'll find you and see that you get the letter.

It is my sad duty to inform you that your father was killed three days ago. Apparently he was kicked in the head by a horse. He was living alone and was found in front of his house, probably a day or more after he was killed. His will leaves the Bar C to you. I also have a letter for you from him.

Conditions are very bad on Skull Mesa these days, with Queen Bess becoming more arrogant as time passes. She does not want a man of your reputation returning to Painted Rock, so she will go to extreme lengths to keep Ernie from finding you, and if she fails in that regard, she will go still farther to keep you from coming back. For that reason I suggest that you arrive in Painted Rock at night and come directly to my house.

Sincerely yours,
Anton Cryder

Clay read the letter through twice, then laid it on the desk. His father's death was not anything for him to grieve over. His mother had died when he was twelve and his father had raised him with considerable help from a leather strap that hung from a nail on the kitchen wall. Now, thinking back, he wondered why he had stayed home those last nine years.

John Roland had been a strong man, strong enough to do two men's work. He had demanded a day's work from Clay even when he had been a small boy. Whatever brightness had been in Clay's life as a child had come from his mother. After her death there had been none.

Clay leaned back in his chair, thinking how it had been before he'd left home. He was twenty-one, old enough to be in love with Linda Stevens. She had been in love with him, too, but he had killed a man on Painted Rock's Main Street and his father had told him he no longer had a home. Not that it made much difference. He would have left anyway, for the situation had become intolerable.

The trouble was he had asked Linda to go with him. He had no money and no job, so he couldn't blame Linda for saying no. Not the way he looked at it now, but at the time he had blamed her. He'd got roaring drunk and left town the next morning with a head as big as a barrel.

If he had any friends, they were back there on Skull Mesa. Bill Land in particular, big and handsome and ambitious. Clay had written to him a few times and it was probably from Land

18

that Cryder had learned he'd been living in Sante Fe. Rusty Mattson, too, who never gave a damn about anything except his freedom. A strange trio, not alike in anything but still held together by the mysterious bonds of friendship. They had gone to school together, they had hunted together and fought and drunk together. More than once they had taken on six of Queen Bess's riders in the Belle Union and whipped them, making a shambles of the saloon.

Clay's friendship with Land and Mattson had added to his troubles with his father, who considered both boys worthless. To John Roland all moral values were black and white with no gray whatever. Strangely enough, Linda Stevens had been on the white side. If Clay had married her before the breakup with his father, he could have brought her to the Bar C and she would have been welcome.

Clay rose and, wadding up the paper, shoved it into his pocket. The decision was not a hard one to make. He was going back. The Bar C was his. He'd run it regardless of Queen Bess. She had always been one to lord it over her neighbors. It probably would be no different now.

If he needed help operating the ranch, he'd get it from Bill Land and Rusty Mattson. Maybe he could hire them to ride for him, and the three of them would be together again. Linda? She had been nineteen when he'd left. She'd be twenty-five now. If she was still single . . . No, that wasn't likely, but at least he could dream.

He went to the bank and withdrew his money, then he turned in his star to the mayor, who objected because he wasn't giving the usual notice. "I've got to go home," Clay said. "I just had word that my father died." With that the mayor shook his hand and wished Clay well.

Home! Clay thought about the word on his way back to the jail. It had seldom been in his thinking for years; the idea that he would ever go back had not been there at all. But it was there now. With his father gone, the Bar C was home. It would never be a big outfit. The range was limited because the Flagg outfit had expanded until the Bar C was surrounded, but it was big enough for Clay, big enough to make a living for him and Linda if she was still single and would marry him. Foolish thinking, he told himself, but it was the way he would think until he learned she was married.

He picked up the few personal things in the marshal's office that belonged to him, then left the building and strode rapidly to the one-room cabin he rented. A place to sleep and to cook his meals. No more, but it had been all he needed. Now he hurriedly packed the things he wanted. Not much to show for six years, he thought. The next six would have to be better.

He rolled up his blankets, filled a flour sack

with bacon and coffee and bread, and picking up his Winchester, started toward the door. He stopped, swearing softly. Blacky Doane was coming toward him across the vacant lot in front of the cabin.

This was a hell of a piece of bad timing, he thought angrily. In five more minutes he'd have saddled his bay gelding and been on his way out of town, heading east across the desert. He had no more official business here; he had nothing against Blacky Doane except that the man had killed Ernie Layton. Maybe the killing couldn't have been helped, but Doane had got down and crawled in the livery stable and it probably had been gnawing at him ever since. Clay knew how it was with a man like that. Once the sand began to run out, there was nothing left unless it was stopped. Doane had to make his try or he was finished.

Clay turned back into his cabin, laid the things that were in his hands on the table, and stepped outside. Doane was thirty feet away. Clay said: "The letter told me my father was dead. I'm going home. I've turned in my star. I don't want any trouble with you, so let it stand."

Doane stopped, his legs spread, the sun almost down behind him. The corners of his mouth were twitching; his right hand, splayed over his gun butt, was trembling.

"Let it stand, you say? You know I can't do

that, Roland. I was paid to keep you from getting that letter. Lavine said they didn't want you to come back. Well, you got the letter, so I've got to keep you from going home."

"We both know the letter's not the reason you came back," Clay said. "Likewise we both know what the reason is. It's not worth your dying for."

"I ain't the one who's going to die!" Doane shouted. "God damn you, I've got to make you stay. The only way to do that is to kill you."

"You aren't fast enough to take me," Clay said. "You knew that in the stable or you wouldn't have caved. I tell you it's not worth it, Doane."

The man shook his head, his face hard-set and stubborn. He said: "Make your play, Roland."

No, it wasn't worth Doane's dying for, Clay told himself, yet he had seen men die for less. For pride. Or shame. Or the fear of going on living with their reputation gone.

Clay took one long step forward, pulling his hat brim lower over his eyes. "You need all the edge you can get, Doane. You've got the sun to your back. You need that, too, so go ahead and pull."

This was adding insult to injury. Doane cursed him, and then, because he had come too far to back down, he made his draw. Clay's hand swept down, lifted the gun from leather, and leveled it. He fired, his bullet hitting Doane in the chest.

Clay felt the hard buck of the walnut handle of the .45 in his hand, saw the powder smoke roll out into the thinning light, heard the roar of the gun. This time it was Blacky Doane who was a split second too slow, his bullet kicking up dust at Clay's feet. He went down in a curling fall, his gun dropping from his hand. He lay quite still in the dust, the harsh sunlight upon him.

Clay stared at Doane's motionless body, sick with regret. He had done all he could to avoid a fight, but it hadn't been enough. According to Anton Cryder's letter, this was only the beginning if he returned to Skull Mesa. But he could not turn back. In that way he was like Blacky Doane. His course was set for him.

Wheeling into the cabin, he picked up the things he had laid on the table, and, walking rapidly to the shed in the rear saddled his horse. A few minutes later the town was behind him. He would never go back to wearing a star. That part of his life was closed out. Six years of it. Too long. Whatever lay ahead would be what he made it.

Chapter Three

Clay rode steadily for three days. He crossed a desert, an empty land covered by tangy sage with hummocks of sand built up around each stalk, the dry branches rattling in the ceaseless wind. He crossed a mountain range covered by cedars and piñons; he camped near the summit in the aspens beside a small stream of clear, sweet water. He smelled the mountain smells, he heard the mountain sounds, and he breathed deeply of the thin, pure air. This was the world of the high country in which he had grown up, and he had missed it more than he had realized.

Late in the afternoon of the third day he started down a long ridge covered by cedars. Other spiny crests tipped up on both sides of him with deep cañons between them. Here and there streaks of red sandstone broke through the black-green of the cedars. These were the Smoky Hills just over the Colorado line from Utah, an outlaw country carefully avoided by men who carried stars.

A few greasy-sack spreads were scattered through the hills. Men settled where they could find water, usually single men, for few women could stand the monotony and the loneliness that this harsh country forced upon them. Most of the men were wanted by the law somewhere. Tired of running, they had settled down to live their lives out in peace.

This was Rusty Mattson's kind of country. Clay had often come here hunting with him, but never with Bill Land, who was afraid of it and its people. Clay had often thought about that because it told him something about the two men. Land had no friends here, but the latchstring was always out for Mattson. Clay was accepted because he was Mattson's friend. It would have been the same for Land if he'd had the courage to come with Mattson and Clay, but he never had.

Ahead of Clay the rim of Skull Mesa was a sharp black line, as straight as if it were a ruler laid against the sky. Beyond that line on the lush grass of the mesa were the Bar C and the Flagg outfit and other ranches and the town of Painted Rock. They were two worlds, Skull Mesa and the Smoky Hills, separated by that rim, and only a few men like Rusty Mattson and Long Sam Kline claimed citizenship in both.

Clay intended to spend the night at Kline's place at the foot of the rim where Storm River cut a gash through the cliff that was nearly a thousand feet high. A road of sorts followed the river to the top, a road barely wide enough for a wagon. It took a good man like Long Sam to bring a loaded wagon down off the mesa. On one side the hubs almost scraped the bank while on the other side they hung over fifty feet of nothing, the boiling water of Storm River directly below them.

Kline ran a combination store, saloon, and roadhouse where the Smoky Hills men bought their supplies and occasionally spent the night if the weather was bad or if they consumed too much of Long Sam's whiskey, which was potent if it wasn't good. The mesa ranchers viewed the Kline establishment with distrust and talked vaguely of raiding the place and destroying it because it was a hang-out for rustlers and outlaws.

On the other hand, the Smoky Hill men hated the mesa people with the deep and passionate hatred that those outside the pale often have for the wealthy and righteous who sit in the seats of the mighty. They said that if Kline's place was destroyed, they'd burn every ranch on the mesa. Clay was convinced that it was this threat more than anything else that had saved Kline's business.

Six years was long enough to dim a man's memory of a country. Somewhere Clay took a wrong trail that brought him off the ridge and down to the river below the Kline place, wasting at least an hour for him. It was dark before he heard the pound of the river in the gorge and saw the lights in the windows of the Kline house ahead of him.

A man stepped out of the shadows as Clay pulled up and dismounted. He asked: "Looking for a place to stay?"

"That's right," Clay said, wondering who the man was. "Got an empty room?"

"You bet." The man leaned forward, peering into the darkness. "You can get a drink and grub inside if you're running low."

"I'll settle for supper and breakfast in the morning," Clay said. "Where'll I put my horse?"

"I'll take him," the man said. "Which way did you come in?"

"From Utah, if it's any of your business," Clay said. Something wasn't right here, Clay thought. As he remembered the place, Long Sam never hired any help. He had a daughter named Ardis who took care of the rooms and the kitchen and served the meals. Kline did everything else.

Caution took hold of Clay. He backed away, asking: "This the Kline place?"

"That's right." The man hesitated, then asked: "You wouldn't be Clay Roland?"

"Long Sam never used to ask questions," Clay said.

"Long Sam's dead," the man said. "Ardis is running the outfit. I'm working for her. Name's Monroe."

"Ardis particular about who she does business with?"

"No, it ain't that." Monroe hesitated again, then

prodded. "You ain't said whether you're Clay Roland."

"I'm Roland," Clay said. "What the hell difference does it make?"

"Difference, he says," Monroe scoffed softly, as if the question made Clay a fool for asking it. "I'll tell you and I'll make it quick. You're close to being a dead man. I don't know you, so I don't give a damn one way or the other, but I'd like to keep Ardis out of trouble. Now I'll tell you what you do. You go into the dining room and stay out of the store side. There's two front doors. I guess you've been here before, so you know which is which."

Monroe would have led the horse away into the darkness if Clay had not grabbed his arm. "This takes a little explaining. Why do you want me to go into the dining room?"

"I'm trying to save your life," Monroe said. "We've been watching for you and now you're here. Do what I tell you."

Anger began building in Clay. "This takes a little more explaining, mister."

"I've told you all I'm supposed to." Monroe jerked free of Clay's grip. "From what I hear, you've got two friends in the whole damned country and you'd better do what you can to keep 'em. Ardis is one. She wants you to come in through the dining room. If she ain't there, go on back to the kitchen."

This time Clay let him go. So Long Sam was dead and Ardis was Clay's friend. He remembered her as a red-headed tomboy who kept the place clean and cooked good meals and could ride as well as most men. She'd been about sixteen or seventeen, he thought. She'd be a woman now, but he didn't know why she was his friend. And who was the other one? Anton Cryder maybe.

Clay hesitated, staring at the windows, then he shrugged. Just as well do as he was told. He stepped up on the porch and opened the door into the dining room. It was empty and the door into the store and bar was closed. He heard pans rattle in the kitchen. He looked at the door into the store and wondered what was on the other side of it that he wasn't supposed to see.

He walked between the tables to the kitchen. A woman was standing at the stove washing dishes, her back to him. She was small, not over five feet tall, the size Ardis had been the last time he had seen her. He remembered her hair as being fiery red, but it was darker now, more auburn than red. She had filled out, too, but that was to be expected, for she had been as slim-bodied as a boy six years ago.

He said: "Ardis."

She whirled, holding her dripping hands in front of her, and stared at him for a moment, her eyes wide. Pretty, he thought, much prettier than he had expected her to be, with the saucy, lively

29

face of a woman who enjoys every moment of life.

"Clay," she said. "Clay, I didn't think you'd ever really come."

She ran to him, wiping her hands on her apron. When she reached him, she threw her arms around him and kissed him on the mouth, then she drew her head back to look at him, her strong young arms still around him.

"It's a funny thing how you keep hoping for something to happen," she said, "and you count the minutes and keep on hoping, and all the time you don't think it ever will." She dropped her arms, and motioned toward the table in the middle of the room. "I'll fix your supper right away. You don't mind eating in here, do you?"

"Of course not, but I want to know something. Your man told me not to go into the store. Why?"

She hesitated, her eyes searching his face as if not quite sure what he would do, then she said: "Abe Lavine's waiting for you in there. I don't want him to know you're here."

"Why?"

"Because . . ." She swallowed, her gaze still fixed on his face, then she forced herself to go on. "Because he'll kill you."

Chapter Four

For a long moment he stared at her, questions pushing at him. Why had she greeted him the way she had? Why was she so anxious to keep him alive? Why was Abe Lavine waiting to kill him? He could guess the answer to that one. Lavine had not been sure Blacky Doane would do the job for which he had been hired. Lavine's presence here was simply insurance that Clay never reached the mesa. He could not think of answers to the other two questions.

He said: "Ardis, did it ever occur to you that I might kill Lavine?"

"Do you know him?"

"No."

"If you knew him, you wouldn't ask that question. About a year ago Queen Bess hired him and a punk kid named Pete Reno. In the year they've been on the mesa, they've killed five men in gunfights in Painted Rock. Pa saw the last one. He said he'd never seen a man as fast as Lavine, and Pa knew a lot of gunmen. Some of the best have stayed here in this house."

Clay nodded, knowing that was right. Long Sam Kline might have been right about Lavine's gun speed, too, but right or wrong, Clay was not a man to duck a fight. If he was going to live on

Skull Mesa, this was a situation that had to be met sooner or later.

"I'd better let Lavine know I'm here," Clay said. He turned toward the dining room.

She cried out: "You can't do this, Clay! You just can't."

He swung back to face her. "Would you think any more of me if I hid here in the kitchen and ate supper, then sneaked upstairs to a bedroom, and sneaked out in the morning without him knowing it?" He shook his head at her. "I don't think you would, Ardis, and I know I'd think a lot less of myself."

This time she let him go. She stood motionlessly beside the kitchen table, her hands clenched at her sides, her face very white. Clay paused before he opened the door into the store and bar, checked his gun, and eased it back into the holster. Turning the knob, he opened the door and stepped into the other room.

Nothing had changed here. He remembered the room well. The store counter was on the side next to the dining room, the shelves behind it filled with staples. A pine bar was on the other side, a bracket lamp on the wall above it. One man stood in the fringe of light at the far end of the bar. Clay moved slowly toward him, feeling the man's probing gaze on him.

"You serve yourself if you want a drink," the man said, "and you lay your money on the bar.

32

The girl who runs this layout thinks everybody is honest."

"I don't want a drink," Clay said. "You're Abe Lavine?"

"I'm Lavine," the man said.

Clay was ten feet from him when he stopped. Lavine was as tall as Clay, and more slender, a barren-faced man with a black mustache, whose feelings and thoughts were secrets known only to himself. His eyes were pale blue, his hair dark brown and thatched with gray at the temples.

Lavine was older than Clay had supposed he was, his sun-blackened skin deeply cut by lines around his eyes and down his cheeks. Forty at least, Clay decided, and possibly even older, a veteran at the gunfighting game. His expressionless eyes, his long, supple fingers, the black-butted gun holstered low on his hip—all this was evidence that he knew his business.

"I'm Clay Roland," Clay said. "They told me you've been waiting for me."

Lavine gave a half-inch nod of agreement. "It ain't been so bad, waiting here. The whiskey is worse than you would believe if I told you, but the girl is a good cook and the bed's all right." He picked up his hat from the bar and put it on his head. "I'll go tell Queen Bess you're here. She'll want to know."

Lavine moved toward the door, passing within three feet of Clay but not looking at him. His

33

back would have been an inviting target for some men. Clay said: "Lavine, you've lived a long time to be this careless."

Lavine turned, a faint smile touching his lips. "I know quite a bit about you, Roland, so it isn't carelessness."

"Maybe not," Clay said. "I didn't suppose you knew that much about me. Maybe you know something else. Why does Queen Bess want to keep me off the mesa?"

"You'll have to ask her. I just work for her."

"Then take a message to her. I'm going to live on the Bar C."

"I'll tell her. Anything else?"

A cold one, Clay thought, this Lavine, and probably as dangerous as Ardis thought. He said: "One more thing. Blacky Doane is dead."

"I'm not surprised," Lavine said. "He never was as fast as he thought he was."

"A kid named Ernie Layton had a letter for me and Doane killed him to keep me from getting it. Why?"

"I wasn't there, so I don't know. I told Doane to keep you from getting the letter, but I didn't tell him to kill the Layton boy. I avoid trouble if I can. The way I figured, it would save a hell of a lot of trouble if you never heard from Cryder. Trouble is it didn't work. Two men are dead. You're going to run the Bar C, and that means more dead men, so I was wrong."

He gave Clay that short nod again, and, turning to the door, opened it and went out. Clay cuffed his hat back and scratched his head. He had been geared for a showdown that hadn't come. He didn't understand it. He returned to the kitchen to find Ardis, standing exactly where he had left her. When she saw him, she pulled a chair back from the table and sat down quickly as if her wobbly knees would no longer hold her.

"I didn't think it would be you," she whispered. "I thought it would be Lavine."

"And I'd make a run for it." He shook his head at her, frowning. "Never run from anything, Ardis. If you run once, everybody hears about it, and they'll figure you'll run again. Chances are you will, too."

She rose. "I'll fix your supper."

He hung his hat on a nail and sat down at the table. "Did he tell you he was going to kill me?"

"No, but everybody around here knew that Anton Cryder had sent for you, and everybody knows Queen Bess won't let you run the Bar C. She's said it often enough and I guess nobody ever heard of her going back on her word. Pete Reno was here for a while watching for you, then he left and Lavine came. If they didn't aim to kill you, why were they here?"

"I sure don't know," he said. "Lavine was real polite. Just told me he'd let Queen Bess know I was here. Said she'd want to know, but I don't savvy why she's so bound to keep me from coming back."

"I don't know." She dropped slices of ham into a frying pan and returned to the table. "There's something else, Clay, something I want you to help me with. Will you?"

"Sure. I'll try anyhow."

She stared down at her hands that were folded on her lap. "Funny how well I remember you, Clay. It seems a long time ago and we were both young. I guess I was just a kid to you, but you weren't a kid to me. Rusty was. He still is in some ways. I don't think he ever will grow up, but it was different with you. I don't know why, but you always gave me the feeling that you were going to do something big and good someday."

He grinned at her. "I never had any such notion in my head."

"Maybe not, but it was what I thought. Rusty says you never had sense enough to be afraid. I guess you're still that way, or you wouldn't have gone after Lavine the way you did." She paused, biting her lower lip, then added: "Clay, I think my father was murdered. I want his killer punished."

"How did he die?"

"His wagon went off the road in the gorge last June. The river was terribly high. We didn't find his body for two days. When we did, it was all chewed up the way it would be in the river. He'd gone to Painted Rock for a load of supplies. He

36

might have been a little drunk. He was sometimes when he came back from town, but drunk or sober, he could bring a wagon down that gorge blindfolded. I just don't believe it could have been an accident."

"Why would anyone kill him?"

She rose and, going back to the range, turned the ham. "For the same reason that mesa bunch has always talked about," she said. "Things have changed since you were here, Clay. For the worse. Did you know that Queen Bess was paralyzed from the waist down and spends her time in a wheelchair?"

He shook his head, shocked by what she had said. He remembered Queen Bess as an active woman who had run her ranch with great skill, an excellent rider who knew as much about the cattle business as any man Clay had ever met. It was impossible to think of her bound to a wheelchair and delegating the responsibility for running the outfit to her foreman, Riley Quinn.

"What happened?" he asked.

"Apparently she was thrown from a horse," Ardis answered. "At least her horse came in and her men found her several hours later between her place and the Bar C. She was unconscious. They got Doc Spears and he brought her around, all right, but she was paralyzed. Not long after that she hired Lavine and Pete Reno. A lot of bad things have happened since then, including the death of your father. Mine, too. I think both of them were murders. Maybe she's gone crazy, sitting there in that chair the way she does."

"Now hold on," Clay said. "What makes you think Dad was murdered?"

"A hunch," she said. "He knew horses as well as Pa knew that gorge road. I don't think he'd let a horse kick him to death any more than Pa would drive off the road."

"But who would do it?" he demanded. "And why?"

"Riley Quinn maybe. Or Lavine, or Reno. I believe Queen Bess ordered it done, but I don't know why. Not your dad. It's easy enough to guess why they killed Pa. They were talking about rustling before you left. There's been a lot more talk lately. Pa got the blame for it."

She forked the ham from the frying pan into a plate and took it to him, then brought bread and a dish of beans from the pantry, and coffee from the stove. He watched her quick, graceful movements, thinking about what she had said.

Ardis was right in saying there had always been talk of rustling and the Smoky Hills men had always been suspected, but Clay doubted that it had ever amounted to much. When there was more winter loss than was expected, a rancher naturally thought of rustling. This was one of the reasons Clay's father had objected to him running with Rusty Mattson, who had been linked with the hills men since he'd been a kid. No one had ever proved anything against him, but Rusty's rootless life naturally brought him under suspicion.

"Where's Rusty?" Clay asked.

She smiled. "Hard to tell. You can find his campfires all through the hills, winter or summer. He comes here often, so I'll see him one of these days. When I do, I'll tell him you're back, and he'll come to the Bar C to see you."

She turned quickly from him and walked to the stove. "Then I suppose they'll kill him. They've posted him off the mesa. They've put posters up all along the rim that say he's got to stay off the mesa. If he doesn't, anyone will be paid five hundred dollars who shoots him or brings him to Painted Rock a prisoner."

"They can't do that. There's no law that says . . ."

"Oh, Clay!" she cried. "Don't you know? There's no law on the mesa except Flagg law? Queen Bess was the one who got Ed Parker appointed marshal in Painted Rock. He never arrests a Flagg hand, but he'll arrest anyone else. He'll arrest you if she says to whether you've done anything or not."

Clay shook his head, unable to believe that Anton Cryder had meant all of this when he had written that conditions were bad on Skull Mesa. He'd see Cryder tomorrow and ask him.

Ardis came to him and put a hand on his

shoulder. "Maybe you don't believe me, Clay, but after you've been here a while you will. I loved my father. He never hurt anyone. In his way he did a lot of good. It just isn't right that his murderer should go unpunished. Will you do something about it?"

He looked at her and nodded. "I'll try," he said, and wondered if he, like Rusty Mattson, would be posted off the mesa.

Chapter Five

Abe Lavine reached the Flagg Ranch sometime after midnight, put his horse away, and slipped into the bunkhouse so quietly that even Pete Reno, who slept across from him, did not wake up. He stared at the dark ceiling, only half hearing the snores of the men, although he was always aware when the foreman, Riley Quinn, rolled over on his back. Quinn was a powerful snorer, but no one complained. Flagg men soon learned that it didn't pay to complain about anything to Quinn.

Lavine's thoughts fastened on Clay Roland. He had wanted to meet Roland for a long time. By Lavine's standards, everything he had heard about Roland had been good. In many ways they were similar. He had been pleased to observe that physically they were somewhat alike. Both had pale blue eyes and brown hair, both were about six feet tall and slender, with Roland having heavier shoulders and arms. Roland was younger, too, maybe twenty-six or twenty-seven.

Lavine was forty-two, old enough to worry about age slowing him up. He had been bothered about this for the last two years, realizing that the years had subtracted just a little from the fine physical co-ordination that had given him the fast draw that had earned him his reputation. Even more important than anything age was doing to him was the fact that he had begun to worry. That was fatal, he knew. This would have to be his last job. That was something else that had worried him. He didn't know what else he could do. Guns had been his life for twenty years or more.

Clay Roland was young enough to have many good years ahead of him, but he was smart to come back to a ranch that belonged to him. Even considering the odds he was bucking, he was still smart. He didn't scare, and that was a big mark on his side of the ledger. It was hard to whip a man who didn't scare. But the main thing was that Clay Roland had something of his own to fight for. That was the big difference between Roland on one side, and Abe Lavine and Pete Reno on the other.

Gunfighters came in all sizes and shapes, each with his own individual code of ethics. It made no real difference that some carried stars and some didn't. Lavine had known lawmen who liked to kill and used their badges to make the killings legal. There were others, like himself, who had never carried a star but lived by a strict code that kept them from killing unless they were forced into a fight.

The star was immaterial. The standard by which a man lived was the important thing. If you knew a little of a man's history, you could make a fair guess as to what his standard was. That was why Lavine had felt perfectly safe in turning his back on Roland at the Kline place; he knew Roland's history for the last six years.

Lavine thought about Pete Reno, who had ridden with him for a couple of years. Reno was only twenty now. He seemed to get worse instead of better. He was somewhat like the Layton kid who had gone down before Blacky Doane's gun, brash and arrogant and too eager. If Reno had been staying at the Kline place when Roland had rode in, he'd have forced a fight and probably have been killed. Lavine wished it had happened. He never should have let the boy throw in with him, but he had, and now it was hard to get rid of him.

Lavine's thoughts returned to Roland again, and he realized with keen regret that fate had put them on opposite sides, that sooner or later he'd be facing Roland with a gun in his hand if he continued to work for Bess Flagg. The smart thing to do would be to quit now, but he liked it here. The pay was good. And he liked Linda Stevens, who worked for Queen Bess. Not that he had any chance with her. She was engaged to marry Bill Land and that was too bad.

The gossip was that Linda had been Clay's girl before he'd left the country and that Land had been Roland's friend. An interesting situation that was loaded with dynamite, he thought, as he dropped off to sleep.

He woke with the crew at dawn. He dressed and shook Pete Reno awake. The boy would sleep through breakfast if Lavine didn't wake him. The cook wasn't one to put himself out cooking an extra breakfast for a kid like Reno. Lavine sat down on his bunk and rolled and smoked a cigarette as Reno rubbed his eyes and yawned. Quinn and the crew had left the bunkhouse.

Reno dressed, still yawning and shaking the cobwebs out of his head. He asked: "Roland show up?"

"He's here," Lavine said.

"Kill him?"

"No."

Reno shot him a quick glance. "Why not?"

"You know our orders," Lavine said. "Come on or we'll go hungry."

They stepped out into the cold dawn light, both men buckling their gun belts about their waists. They found seats at the end of the long table, Riley Quinn and the crew ignoring them. This was the way it always went, for the two of them were set apart from the others. All of them, Riley Quinn in particular, resented their presence.

Lavine drowned his flapjacks with syrup as he considered Quinn. He guessed he wasn't as happy here as he kept telling himself. He certainly had no reason to like Quinn. The foreman was a squat

44

man, five feet six or so, and almost as wide as he was tall, with a neck that reminded Lavine of an oak anchor post and a temper that resembled a buzz saw.

Glancing at him, Lavine noticed that a stubborn lock of hair had fallen across his forehead. Impatiently Quinn swept it back with a big hand and went on eating. He wasn't a good foreman in Lavine's opinion. He was too hard on his men, too unyielding on any question on which he had made up his mind.

Quinn was fanatically loyal to the Flagg outfit and to Queen Bess personally, a characteristic which did nothing to improve Lavine's opinion of him. Loyalty alone wouldn't keep him from making a mistake. Being the kind of man he was, any mistake he made would be a whopper.

The crew drifted out, spurs jingling. Reno looked at Lavine when the last man had left. He said: "Sometimes I wonder how long it would take him to break the neck of a man like you or me."

"Or Clay Roland," Lavine added.

Reno nodded, grinning. "There's a neck he'd enjoy breaking."

"No more than yours or mine," Lavine said. "He was sore the day Queen Bess hired us and he's been sore ever since. He'll keep on being sore until she fires us, figuring that there's nothing we can do he can't."

"Maybe there ain't," Reno said. "I sure don't savvy why you didn't plug Roland when you had a chance."

Lavine finished his coffee. He glanced at the boy's pimply face, the pouting lower lip, the green eyes, and shook his head as he rose. "I never learned you nothing," he said. "I'm not sure whether I'm a bad teacher or you're stupid."

He went out into the early morning sunshine, glancing southward at the sandstone cliffs on the other side of town from which Painted Rock got its name. At midday they were maroon, but at this hour when the sun rose into a clear sky, they changed to a fiery red. To Lavine they were beautiful, even a source of strength at times. He never quite understood how that was, but it was true, although he never mentioned it to anyone.

He drifted across the dusty yard to the corrals where Quinn was giving the orders for the day. Reno caught up with him, saying petulantly: "I ain't going to be called stupid."

"Can I help it if you act stupid?"

"You're scared of him," Reno said.

"Don't tell anyone," Lavine said. "I sure don't want it to get out."

The men began riding off. Quinn wheeled his horse toward Lavine and reined up, his big head tipped forward so that his eyes raked Lavine. He said: "I guess Roland showed up or you wouldn't be here."

"That's right," Lavine said.

"You tell him to stay off the mesa?"

Lavine shook his head. "My orders were to tell Missus Flagg if he showed up. That's what I'll do."

Even after working out of doors for years, Quinn's face was not tanned by the high country sun. Instead it burned, with the result that his skin was red and constantly peeling. Now it turned scarlet as quick anger boiled up in him. "By God, I wish I could give you an order once in a while. I'd work your tail off."

"I guess you would." Lavine grinned as the foreman whirled his horse and raked him cruelly with his spurs. He nodded at Reno. "We're about done here, Pete. Either we go or Quinn goes."

"We ain't going," Reno said. "This is too good a job."

"Maybe," Lavine said. "Maybe not. Well, I'd better go see the boss."

He turned toward the big ranch house, wondering whatever had possessed old Hank Flagg to make him build a sprawling, two-story house like this. It had happened years ago, but Lavine had heard the gossip in Painted Rock often enough. Twenty years or more ago Hank Flagg had married Bess and brought her here. He had built the house over her objections, telling her brusquely it was her wedding present. Hank had lived three years and died, leaving Bess the ranch with a house she didn't want. Now the outfit was twice what it had been in Hank's day, and according to the talk in Painted Rock, Bess was twice the man Hank had been.

Lavine went around to the back of the house where he knew Queen Bess would be having breakfast, and knocked. She called: "Come in!" He opened the door and stepped inside, nodding at Ellie, a Negro woman who kept house for Bess, and went on to the table where Linda Stevens sat beside Bess.

"Have a cup of coffee, Lavine," Queen Bess said in her big voice. "Ellie, fetch him a cup."

"Yes, ma'am," Ellie said, and brought a cup and the coffee pot to the table.

"Thank you, I will," Lavine said, and dropped into a chair across from Linda as Ellie filled his cup.

"Good morning, Mister Lavine," Linda said.

"I hadn't noticed if it was a good morning or not," Lavine said. "I guess it is, though."

"What's the matter?" Bess asked. "Have trouble with Roland?"

Lavine shook his head. "A short night. That's all. He got in after dark, so I was late getting here."

He glanced at Bess, who had rolled her wheelchair back from the table and was studying him intently. Even at forty she was a handsome woman. In spite of her big voice and large, capable hands, she was very much a woman, and he thought he would have liked to have seen her before her accident.

He said slowly: "This Roland seemed to be all right. Why don't you let him . . . ?"

"Lavine, I'm surprised at you," she broke in. "Clay Roland will never work the Bar C. It doesn't even exist. It's part of Flagg range. Did you tell him that?"

"No. He gave me a message for you. He said he was going to work the Bar C."

"You're a fool, Lavine. That's when you should have killed him."

He was always shocked at the change that came over Bess when she talked about Clay Roland. Ordinarily she seemed a pleasant woman who was easy to get along with as long as she wasn't crossed. She seldom was. In the year he had been here, he had watched her hatred for John Roland grow until it had become a poison in her. After his death she had fastened that hatred on Clay.

He shook his head at her, not liking the darkness that flowed across her face, the ugly way her mouth tightened against her teeth. He said: "No, I'm not a fool. Two weeks ago we decided how to play this. It was the right way. Don't change it now."

She tapped her fingers on the arms of her wheelchair, staring at him in the strange, blank way she always did when they talked about Clay

Roland. It was as if she was seeing Roland in her mind and not Abe Lavine.

"We will change it," she said. "We'll post him off the mesa the way we did Mattson. Somebody else will kill him. If they don't, we will. I want you to go to town and have the posters printed today. Tomorrow you and Reno see they're put up."

"You have no grounds for that," he said.

"Suspicion of rustling is all the grounds I need," she snapped. "Everybody knows he used to run with Mattson. If Mattson steals cattle, so will Roland."

"No, it's different with Roland," Lavine said. "Folks know about him. He has a reputation as a lawman. I heard about him a long time before I came here. It's easy enough to pin a rustling charge on a drifter like Mattson, but you can't do it with Roland."

She leaned forward, her hands gripping the arms of her chair so hard the knuckles turned white. "Lavine, are you telling me my business?"

"No ma'am," Lavine said. "This is my business. You're paying for my experience as well as my gun. I wouldn't be earning my pay unless I gave you some suggestions."

She leaned back in her chair. "All right, Lavine. Let's hear your suggestions."

This irritated him, for they had covered the ground carefully two weeks ago before he had hired Blacky Doane to see that Cryder's letter never reached Clay Roland. Now there was nothing to do but go over it again.

"You've got to figure out how to deal with each case," he said. "Nobody cares whether Rusty Mattson is posted off the mesa or not except his friends out there in the hills. He's smart enough to stay off. It's different with Clay Roland. The sheriff may live a hundred miles from here, but he's heard about Roland. So has the governor. If this isn't handled just right, somebody, Anton Cryder maybe, will send for the sheriff. Or write to the governor. You don't want either one to happen."

"Why not?"

He picked up his cup of coffee and drank it, wondering why she would ask a question she could answer as well as he could. He put the cup down. "You know why."

"I want to hear you say it."

"Missus Flagg, I've seen operations like this before. In the long run the pattern is the same. People stand for it for a while. They grumble but they stand for it. Then something happens that's a little too much for 'em to stomach. They'll holler for help from anybody who'll give it. Maybe the sheriff comes and rolls back the rug. He starts at the corner and keeps rolling and pretty soon the whole thing comes out into the open."

"Nobody can prove anything," she said harshly.

"It's not always a matter of proof," he said. "It's more a proposition of somebody fitting the parts together."

"I see. So we've got to wait until we see the right method of handling Roland. That it?"

"That's the size of it. Maybe it'll take a month. Six months. A year. You've got plenty of time."

"That's where you're wrong. I'm not waiting any six months. Or even one month. You're going to town this morning and get those posters printed. We'll hold them till it's time to put them up or something else comes along that looks better." She nodded at Linda. "Hitch up the buggy and take Linda with you. She hasn't been to town for a long time."

Lavine glanced at Linda as he rose.

She nodded and said: "I'd like to go with you if you don't mind."

"My pleasure," he said, and left the kitchen.

Linda was ready by the time he brought the buggy to the front of the house. She stepped into the seat, smiling at him. She was a tall, willowy woman, with black hair and dark brown eyes that were expressive. She was pretty enough, but not too pretty. That was one of the things he liked about her. He had known too many women who were in love with their own beauty.

"I didn't particularly want to go to town," she said, "but I did want to talk to you. How did Clay look?"

"Fine. He's a good man. He deserves a chance to live here in peace."

"You liked him, didn't you?"

He nodded. "Funny thing. I don't usually cotton to a man the first time I see him."

"It's too bad," she said bitterly. "Sooner or later you'll kill him, won't you? Or he'll kill you."

"Maybe not. I don't know how much longer I'll keep this job. Quinn's getting pretty ringy."

"Quit it now, Mister Lavine," she cried. "Right now."

"Why?"

She looked toward the mountains to the east, their slopes still dark with morning shadows. She said slowly: "Did she have you kill Long Sam Kline and John Roland?"

"No. That's not my style."

"But she did have them killed, didn't she?"

"I think so. I couldn't swear to it."

"Don't you see what will happen? You'll be the sacrificial lamb if Queen Bess has to offer one. Riley Quinn is her man. He'd do anything for her, and she'll save him regardless of how many others she throws to the wolves."

"It could work that way," he said. "People around here naturally think the worst of me." He glanced at her, wondering why she kept on working for Queen Bess and why she had ever accepted Bill Land's proposal of marriage. He said: "I guess you want to see Roland."

"I'd like to," she said.

He thought about that all the way into Painted Rock, finally deciding that Linda would never have accepted Land if she had known Roland was coming back. Seeing him today would be a mistake, but he couldn't think of any way to stop it. All he could see ahead was trouble, and both he and Linda were caught right in the big middle of it. He wished he could tell her how he felt about her, but that would be stupid, telling a woman seventeen years younger than he was that he loved her.

Then the bitterness took hold of him. It wasn't the years; it was the life he had lived. He would not make any woman a fit husband. Even if he had a chance with her, he couldn't tell her. He wanted to put his arms around her, to feel her young body against his, but he looked straight ahead, holding himself under tight discipline. She might as well have been a mile away.

Chapter Six

Clay left the Kline place after breakfast, telling Ardis he would be back as soon as he could and for her to keep Rusty Mattson off the mesa. Rusty couldn't do any good now. He'd just get himself killed. Ardis agreed, although she wasn't sure that wild horses could keep Rusty off the mesa once he'd heard that Clay was back.

Halfway up the gorge Clay dismounted and looked over the edge of the shelf road at the rumbling river below him. This was where Long Sam Kline had gone over. The river was low now, but during the spring run-off it was a swollen monster, overflowing its banks on the mesa and then roaring down this narrow cañon as it ate at its imprisoning walls and sent boulders as big as houses thundering down the full length of the gorge.

There was nothing to see now, of course, not even a trace of the wagon or the horses in the cañon below Clay. He wished he had been here when Kline was first missed. He might have found something then. From experience he knew that the best-disguised plan for murder always leaves traces behind it if a man searches carefully enough. But the chances were that no one had looked.

He mounted and rode on, thinking about it and about his father's death. He could not see a good motive for the murder of either one. But there was much he didn't know. He wondered if Bill Land or Anton Cryder would talk freely to him. Or Linda Stevens. He had not asked Ardis about her and Ardis had failed to mention her. That was the first thing he would ask Cryder.

He reached the mesa a few minutes later and went on up the river toward the Bar C. The road to Painted Rock ran parallel to the stream, the ridges on both sides of the small valley cutting off the view except for the San Juan Mountains that lifted above the horizon far to the east, a saw-tooth line of granite peaks that raked the sky.

An hour later he reached the Bar C. He rode slowly now, old memories crowding his mind. His gaze swung from one building to another, and then to the long, narrow hay fields that lay on both sides of the river.

Nothing had changed, he thought, except that there had always been Bar C cattle around, grazing on the ridges or the fields among the haystacks. None was in sight now. No horses in the corral. No dog to bark a welcome. Not even an old hen scratching around the barn and sheds. His father had always kept a few Plymouth Rocks because he liked fresh eggs.

He dismounted in front of the house, leaving the reins dragging. He felt a strange, unfamiliar ache in his chest. This was home, but it wasn't home. Just a deserted ranch house, the front door open. No smoke rising above the chimney, no sign of life anywhere.

He drew his gun and strode up the path to the door, suddenly realizing that if Queen Bess wanted him killed, she might have stationed one of her men inside to shoot him when he stepped through the door. Instead of going in, he wheeled sharply and, ducking under the windows, ran around to the back and went into the kitchen. No one was there.

He crossed to the front room, his boot heels making sharp echoing sounds on the floor. He searched the bedrooms, glanced into the closets, and then, returning to the kitchen, looked into the pantry. The house was empty.

He holstered his gun, feeling foolish although he knew that his suspicion of an ambush had not been caused by any sudden jangling of nerves. It had been a very real possibility. He prowled through the house again, going first into the bedroom that had been his. As far as he could tell, it had not been touched in the six years he had been gone. The bed was made up, and that raised the thought that perhaps his father had expected him to come back sometime. His clothes were still in the bureau drawers. A pile of toys and other boyhood possessions were in the closet. He remembered his father had asked him several times to go through it and throw away the things he didn't want, but he never had.

Back in the kitchen he saw that the woodbox was full, a pile of kindling on the floor beside it. His father had been methodical that way, seeing to it that there was always enough kindling to start another fire if the one in the big range went out.

The table was clean except for the coating of dust upon the red-and-white oilcloth. The pantry shelves were stacked with cans and sacks of food. Here again his father had been methodical, always laying in a month's supply of food in case a bad storm made the trip to town impossible.

His father hadn't changed and never would if he had lived another twenty years. Clay felt this even more strongly in the front room with its leather couch and potbellied heater, the claw-footed table with the chessmen set alongside the board, the whites on one side, the blacks on the other.

Anton Cryder had likely been here not long before the accident and they'd played a few games, maybe spending a full Sunday afternoon at the chessboard. It was the one relaxation his father had had, and the games were usually nip and tuck between him and Cryder.

Clay remembered that Queen Bess used to visit with them, although he seldom stayed home when she was here. His father had laughed when he'd told Clay how he had taught Bess to play chess, but after a few games she refused to play more. She hadn't won any. She couldn't stand losing, even something as unimportant as a game of chess.

Suddenly the echoing emptiness of the house got to him. He couldn't stay here, not even long enough to cook a meal. He couldn't stand it, living by himself the way his father had for six years. He would have welcomed Rusty Mattson's company, even knowing the danger it meant to Rusty.

He closed the window and the doors and, mounting, rode on up the river toward Painted Rock. He'd find out about Linda. Maybe he could get Bill Land to come out and stay with him for a while. He had forgotten to ask Ardis about Land. He had no idea what his friend was doing, but he remembered that Land had never been much on hard work if there was any other way to make a living. He'd be company even if he didn't work. Or maybe Anton Cryder could find a good man who needed a job.

Clay tried to make plans as he rode. The cattle were gone, probably driven out of the country as soon as his father's death had become known. The horses were gone, too. Well, he'd have to buy a small herd and a few horses.

Then he shook his head. Foolish thinking, he told himself. The first thing was to prove he could live on the Bar C with someone or alone if he had to. He had no idea what Queen Bess would do, but he had no doubt she would make her move soon.

He climbed steadily. Gradually the slopes on both sides of the valley flattened out and he could see for miles across the rolling mesa, the Flagg buildings making a lump on the horizon north of town. The red cliffs that gave Painted Rock its name lifted sharply above the mesa to his right. Farther to the south were the Snow Mountains, and on his left to the north was the long, aspen-covered ridge known as the Divide. This was Flagg summer range, the best in the country, and he could be reasonably sure that Queen Bess hadn't given up an acre of it.

He reached Painted Rock at noon, seeing a little, piddling town with no more than two dozen buildings spilled out here on the mesa. It was Queen Bess's town as surely as the Flagg Ranch was hers.

As a boy it had seemed a city, but to Clay Roland, the man, coming back after six years, it was nothing, yet he sensed that it was filled with all the evil that would be spawned from hate and greed and arrogance. He still didn't know the reason why so much of it should be aimed at him, but maybe Queen Bess had reached the place where whim instead of reason dictated her actions.

He passed the stable, the tar-papered shack that housed the Painted Rock *Weekly Courier* across the street from it. Some vacant, weed-covered lots, then the Belle Union, the hotel, the bank, and Doc Spears's drugstore. He glanced at the upstairs window of the drugstore and shock hit him like a hard fist in his stomach. Letters painted on the glass read: *William Land, Attorney at Law*.

He reined up in front of Walters's Mercantile and dismounted and tied, his gaze still on the sign. So Bill Land was a lawyer. Clay knew he shouldn't have been surprised. Land would be a good lawyer by some standards—big, handsome, glib-tongued, and not too particular about how he made a dollar.

When Clay had been a kid running around with Land and Rusty Mattson, these things hadn't been important, but they were now, and the truth jolted Clay. Six years had done this, three boys who had gone three separate ways and had become men. Looking back, Clay could see why his father had felt the way he had about the other two.

Anton Cryder's office was over the Mercantile. Clay turned toward the outside stairway that led to the second floor of the building. Funny how Bill Land's sign, the one thing on Painted Rock's Main Street which was different, had given Clay's thoughts a new turn.

Lawyers were the same as other men. Some were honest and some were crooks. Cryder was one of the honest ones. Nothing would ever change him. Clay was ashamed of his thoughts about Land, yet he could not escape the conviction that the man who had been his friend was the exact opposite of Anton Cryder.

He was halfway up the stairs when he heard heels pound on the boardwalk in front of the Mercantile, then a woman's voice called: "Clay!"

He glanced back. Linda Stevens stood there, her head tipped back, her dark eyes shining as she said: "Clay, I was hoping I would see you."

For a moment he didn't move. His heart suddenly began doing crazy things in his chest so he couldn't breathe. This was Linda in the flesh, an older and mature Linda, but still the girl he had loved when he'd left, and now he told himself he had never quit loving her.

"Clay, what's the matter with you?" she asked. "Aren't you glad to see me?"

He moved then, rushing down the stairs to her. "Glad?" he shouted. "I was never gladder to see anyone in my life than I am you."

She started to back away as if frightened by something she saw in his face, but he would not be put off. He grabbed her in both arms and picked her up and whirled her around. "Clay, put me down!" she cried. "Put me down. You're a madman."

"Sure I am," he said.

He put her down and kissed her, never thinking he should ask if she was married. For a moment she resisted him, her lips stiff and cool, then resistance fled and it was the way it used to be, her mouth sweet and eager, her long, willowy body melting against his.

The street had been deserted a moment before, but it wasn't now. A big hand caught Clay's shoulder and whirled him around, another hand slapped Linda across the face, slamming her against the store wall.

Bill Land said: "By God, I'll kill you for that. She doesn't belong to you now."

A fist caught Clay flush on the jaw, a hard blow that jolted him and sent a flow of stars dancing before his eyes. His feet went out from under him and he sat down hard, his head ringing. He looked up into Land's fury-filled face, and he saw murder written there as clearly as he had ever seen it on the face of any man.

Chapter Seven

Clay was momentarily dazed. He could see and hear, but he couldn't move. Bill Land was reaching into a coat pocket for a gun, deliberately as if he had all the time in the world. Watching him, Clay had the nightmarish feeling that he could do nothing but sit here and take Land's bullet.

He heard the pound of a man's boots on the boardwalk, then Lavine's voice: "Land, I'll kill you if you pull that gun." Linda flung herself at Land and tried to grab his right arm, but he struck her on the side of the head, a hard blow that spun her away from him and almost knocked her down.

Clay came unstuck then. Lavine was still twenty feet away when Clay got to his feet and lunged at Land just as a small gun appeared in Land's right hand. Land swung his left as he backed up, a futile blow that missed by a foot, and then Clay was on him. He had never been as crazy angry before in his life and he had never hit a man harder. His right was a looping uppercut that caught Land flush on the jaw and swiveled his head half around. He followed with a left that smashed Land's nose and brought a spurt of blood.

"Use your gun on him, Roland!" Lavine yelled. "He was going to kill you."

Clay heard the words, but their meaning didn't get through to him. He couldn't think of anything except beating Bill Land into a helpless mass of flesh. The unfairness of the attack, the totally irrational and stupid attempt at murder from a man he had once called his friend, a man he had looked forward to seeing again, all this combined to turn Clay into a fighting maniac.

Land dropped the gun into the dust and kept backing into the street, unable to defend himself against Clay's furious attack. He pawed at Clay; he tried to keep his hands up in front of his face, and when he did, Clay lowered his blows to the man's heart and stomach. Land was never able to regain his balance; he was on the defensive and Clay kept him there, the sound of his blows meaty thuds that could be heard the length of the block.

Unable to stand Clay's punishing blows to his body, Land lowered his forearms to protect his stomach, then Clay caught him with a swinging right to the chin, and Land went down. Standing over him, Clay said: "Get up, Bill. Or have the law books made you so soft you're whipped already?"

Land got to his hands and knees. One eye was almost shut, his lower lip was split and bleeding, and his nose was a mass of jellied meat and blood. He tried to get to his feet, but the strength wasn't in him. His arms broke at the elbows and he fell flat on his face into the dust.

Land rolled over on his side, saying thickly: "I'll kill you for this, Clay. By God, I'll kill you."

Clay backed off, panting and sweaty and sick at his stomach. It was more than Bill Land's battered body lying in the dust in front of him that made him sick; it was the end of a dream he had cherished through all the long miles from Paiute City to Painted Rock.

Clay whirled and walked away as Linda's voice came to him: "I'm sorry, Clay. I'm engaged to marry Bill."

Men had rushed out of their places of business to watch the fight, men Clay had once known well. Bud Walters who owned the Mercantile, Doc Spears, Link Melton from the Belle Union— men who should be welcoming him home and shaking his hand, but they only stared at him in sullen silence. He could not mistake what he saw in their faces. They might as well have said in words that they wished he'd stayed away.

Clay reached the foot of the stairs when Lavine caught up with him. He said: "You're good with your fists, Roland. Real good for a man who has a reputation as a gunfighter."

Clay stopped and turned to face Lavine. The man was friendly, if expressionless neutrality could be called friendly. Clay said: "Maybe that reputation is something I won't need around here."

"You'll need it," Lavine said grimly. "What shape are your hands in?"

Clay held them up and closed them into fists and opened them and closed them again. "Knuckles skinned up a little. That's all."

"You were foolish," Lavine said. "You're too good a man to go under because you've bunged up your hands on a bonehead like Bill Land."

"My hands are all right," Clay murmured, staring at his closed fists. "I'm going to be working cattle. There's plenty of things that can happen to a man's hands when he's on a ranch." He lifted his gaze to Lavine's thin, saturnine face. "Which side are you on?"

"An interesting question," Lavine said as if not quite sure himself. "I think I'm on the wrong side."

Lavine wheeled away to where Doc Spears and Linda were kneeling in the dust beside Land. When Land saw him, he said bitterly: "You threatened to kill me."

"You know why?" Lavine asked. "I guess you wouldn't, so I'll tell you. If you'd shot Roland when he was lying there half knocked out, nobody could have saved you from a hanging, not even Bess Flagg."

Clay turned and climbed the stairs. So Bill Land, attorney, belonged to Queen Bess. Well, he should have guessed that, too. Was there anything on Skull Mesa she didn't own?

He opened the door to Anton Cryder's office and went in. The lawyer had been standing by the window, watching the street. Now he turned, and Clay, seeing his face, deeply lined and as gray as ancient parchment, realized that these six years had been long ones for Anton Cryder.

The old man was very thin and apparently he had a catch in his back that kept him from standing erect. One of the things Clay remembered about him was the ramrod-like posture that had seemed remarkable for a man in his late sixties.

"You're a fool, Clay," Cryder said as he crossed the room and offered his hand.

Clay shook hands with him. "A lot of people seem to think that," he admitted.

"I wrote to you to come to my house at night," Cryder said, "but no, you couldn't do anything that was intelligent and safe. You show up at noon as bold as brass, riding down Main Street so everybody'll see you, you kiss another man's girl, and then you beat hell out of him. If you could have done anything to make your score worse with Queen Bess, I guess you'd have done it."

"Could it be any worse?"

Cryder's liver-brown lips curled in a smile. "Now that you mention it, I guess it couldn't." He motioned to a chair. "Sit down. You're looking well. I'd say Land never laid a fist on you." He chuckled softly, and added: "I've been waiting for quite a while to see somebody make hash out of Bill Land. I enjoyed watching it."

Clay sat down and rolled a smoke, thinking that Cryder was right in calling him a fool. But playing the safe, sly game was not his style. In the long run, the direct way of meeting trouble was the best for him. He wouldn't have done anything differently if he could have gone back and lived the last hour over.

"So Linda's going to marry Bill," Clay said.

"That's what Bill says," Cryder agreed, "but there's a funny thing about it. She works for Queen Bess, you know. Sort of a companion as I get it. Land is Bess's fair-haired boy, about like Riley Quinn. I guess Linda is engaged to him, all right, but he can't seem to get her to the altar even with Bess's help."

"You're saying she doesn't love him?" Clay demanded.

"Hell, how would I know who she loves?" Cryder grunted. "All I'm saying is that Land hasn't been able to get the knot tied, which doesn't mean you can move in and take her away from him. A lot of folks on the mesa like being on the winning side. It's safer. Maybe Linda's like that. Anyhow, it would be a hell of a thing to marry her just so she could be a widow the next day."

"You talk like I was whipped already," Clay said irritably. "Well, I'm not."

"No, but you will be," Cryder said. "You're a good man, Clay. We've heard a lot about you since you left." He opened a drawer and took out a long envelope. "Here is your dad's will and a letter he wrote a month or so ago. I haven't read the letter. Maybe he's told you he was proud of you, but he was a hard-headed man. Backing up on anything he ever said was a tough thing for him to do, so maybe he didn't. But he was proud of you. You can take my word for that."

Cryder laid the envelope on his desk and, picking up his pipe, filled it and fished in his vest for a match. "I'm sure you're a brave man, Clay. Likewise you're a fighting man, but any way I count you, you're still only one man. The odds are too long against you. What you don't know is that there isn't anyone on the mesa you can count on to help you. I would if I could, but you need fighting help, and I'm too sick and old for that."

Clay nodded and flipped his cigarette stub into the spittoon, then reached for tobacco and paper and rolled another one. After what had happened just now, he believed what Cryder told him. It wasn't just Bill Land. It was all the others—Ed Parker and Link Melton and the rest, men he had liked and who had liked him in the old days for all of his wildness, but a few minutes ago they had looked at him as if he were a carrier of typhoid fever.

"Queen Bess came to see me the other day," Cryder went on. "You knew she's paralyzed?"

Clay nodded. "I stopped at Kline's place last night. Ardis told me."

"She couldn't get her wheelchair up my stairs, so she sent that gunslick Lavine to tell me to come down. I thought she had some legal business for me, but I should have known better. She gives all of it to Land and passes the word for everybody else to do the same."

Cryder scowled at the filled bowl of his pipe. "That's a hell of a thing, Clay. I've been here ever since they laid the chunk. For years I was the only lawyer within fifty miles. Whatever legal business there was, I had it. Well, Bill Land went to Montrose, read law in Judge Zale's office, and came back here and put out his shingle. Now I don't get any work. If I didn't have some savings, I'd starve to death."

Anton Cryder had never been a bitter man, but Clay saw the bitterness that was in his face now, the bitterness of an old man who has been made useless through no fault of his own.

"Well, she told me to tell you, if you showed up, that she would pay you one thousand dollars for the Bar C, lock, stock, and barrel, and you were to keep on riding. I thought I'd tell you before you read your dad's letter. Now she didn't say what she'd do if you turned down her offer, but you can guess. She's always been a strong-willed, driving kind of woman, but after she got hurt and Doc Spears told her she'd never get any better, she got mean. Crazy mean. If you stay, she'll get you killed, one way or the other."

Cryder handed the envelope to Clay. "The will is short and simple. Everything goes to you. A quarter-section of deeded land where the buildings are, the cattle and horses, and the cash in the bank. Not much. Less than a thousand dollars."

"I've known men to die for less," Clay said.

He read the will that was as short and simple as Cryder had said, then he tore the envelope open that was marked *Clay*. He glanced at the smooth, flowing handwriting that he remembered so well, handwriting that was as easily read as printing. Clay rose and, walking to the window, stood with his back to Cryder as he read the letter.

Dear Clay,
You will not be reading this letter unless I am dead. Right now my health is perfect, but violence has a way of taking lives in this country and I have a feeling that I will not live very long. Everything I have goes to you, of course. I hope you will live on the Bar C and keep it up as I have, but do not consider this the binding

request of a dead man. Do whatever your best judgment dictates.

I am writing this letter for only one reason. I want to tell you that after all these years I realize I was wrong when I sent you away. I am proud of the record you have made as a lawman. A wild country like the West needs men like you. I will not try to explain why I sent you away. At the time the reasons seemed good. The truth was I thought you would go away and get the wildness out of your system, but you didn't. Perhaps it is better this way. I don't know. I do know I'm lonely and I would like to see you. If you decide to make the Bar C your home, I hope you will be as happy as I was when your mother was alive.

Your father,
John Roland

Clay folded the paper and slipped it back into the envelope. For the first time in his life he had a feeling of sympathy for his father that he'd never had when John Roland was alive. As he turned to face Cryder, he said gravely: "I would have come back if he had written this to me when he was alive."

"He couldn't bring himself to do it," Cryder said. "He was my best friend, but I knew his good qualities as well as his faults. He was a hard man in many ways and maybe a foolish one for not surrendering and writing to you, but I don't think he could."

"I'm not any more anxious to die than the next man," Clay said, "but you tell Bess Flagg I don't want her one thousand dollars. I'm staying."

"I thought you would," Cryder said, "being John's son. I'll do anything I can for you, Clay. Don't forget that. It's just a question of whether you can use what I have to offer."

"Ernie Layton is dead," Clay said, and told him what had happened in Paiute City.

Cryder puffed hard on his pipe, hiding his face behind a cloud of tobacco smoke. A long minute passed before he could control his emotions enough to say: "I sent that boy to his death."

"It wasn't your fault," Clay said. "He played it like a fool. He saw me standing in front of the jail. He must have known I'd be the marshal because from the time he started tracing me he would have heard I was a lawman, but he didn't stop. He just wanted to make a show of finding me, I guess."

"I still sent him to his death," Cryder said.

He would torture himself over this as long as he lived, Clay thought, whether it was his fault or not. Clay changed the subject with: "Ardis Kline told me she thought her father was murdered."

Cryder nodded. "I wouldn't be surprised. You

know the talk about the Smoky Hills boys rustling mesa cattle. Later on it got worse and Kline was blamed for it because they hung around his place. Riley Quinn is a brutal son-of-a-bitch. It's a good bet that he talked Queen Bess into getting rid of Kline. Not that it would have been hard."

Clay sat down again. He had laid the last cigarette he'd rolled on the corner of the desk. Now he picked it up and lit it, then he said: "Ardis told me she thinks Dad was murdered, too."

Cryder nodded again. "I wouldn't be surprised at that, either. A couple of Flagg men found him and brought his body to town. I drove out there and looked around, but I was at least twenty-four hours too late to find anything. Some horse tracks were in front of the house, but they didn't prove anything. I asked Doc Spears about it, but I didn't get any satisfaction out of him. He wouldn't tell me if he knew. The side of John's head was caved in, but I couldn't tell from looking at it whether the injury was from a beating with a club or the kick of a horse."

Clay leaned back in his chair, frowning, the cigarette dangling from one corner of his mouth. "Why did Queen Bess do it? And why is she so set on keeping me from living here?"

"I'll tell you, but I don't think you'll believe me," Cryder said. "She was in love with John, but he wouldn't marry her."

75

Clay jerked the cigarette out of his mouth. He shouted: "By God, Anton, that's the craziest thing I ever heard!"

"It's the truth," Cryder said, "crazy or not. It's not so hard to understand, either. John was a handsome man, the kind that would appeal to a woman like Bess. She's been a widow for a long time. She had no interest in men who ran after her. John didn't, and that challenged her, so she ran after him. It's public knowledge, though I doubt anyone else would tell you. After you left, she just about hounded John to death. He could have had a good life with her if he could have let himself be bossed, but he couldn't. Besides, he loved your mother. After she died, there was never another woman for him.

"Well, Bess would go over there and cook for him. She stayed late at night and he couldn't get her to leave. Finally she got to coming during the night. She tried her damnedest to seduce him. Once she undressed in front of him. I don't know whether she ever made the grade or not, but she might have. She was a fine-looking woman before she got hurt and John was a lonely man. Anyhow, he wouldn't marry her.

"About a year ago they had a fight. Bess couldn't stand being put off any longer. She lost her temper and hit him, and he pushed her out of the house and locked the door. Being Bess Flagg, she went clean crazy, I guess. She got on her horse and rode out of the yard like a rocket. Somewhere between there and her place she got thrown. She still went to see him, making Lavine lift her into the wagon seat, then he'd put the chair in the bed of the wagon. She kept telling John he was to blame. Somewhere along the line she got to hating him. Maybe she decided that if she couldn't have him, nobody else would."

Clay got up and dropped the cigarette that had gone cold into the spittoon. "What about me?"

"Your name's Roland," Cryder answered. "She hates anyone who has that name. Being John's son, you're all that's left of him." Cryder shook his head. "Maybe it's more than that, though. A lot of people hereabouts hate her. You won't hear any of them talking about it, but they hate her, all right. Those two gunslicks she hired make it worse. Riley Quinn doesn't help, either. It might be that a man with your reputation could be a leader who would make big trouble for her. She's not going to take that risk."

Clay slipped his father's letter into his pocket and turned toward the door. Cryder asked: "What are you going to do?"

"I'm going to live on the Bar C," Clay answered.

"You can't go out there now," Cryder said. "They'll raid the Bar C and kill you. Stay here in town with me for a few days."

"Would tomorrow be any better to move out there?" Clay asked. "Or the day after tomorrow? I don't think so, Anton." He nodded at Cryder and left the lawyer's office.

Chapter Eight

Clay ate dinner in the hotel dining room, ignoring the curious stares that were fixed on him. After he finished eating, he stepped into Doc Spears's drugstore in the vague hope that he could persuade the medico to tell him more than he had told Cryder about his father's death, but the doctor wasn't in.

"He's upstairs fixing Bill Land's nose," Mrs. Spears said. "You don't look sick to me. Don't bother Doc unless you are."

"Thank you kindly, ma'am," Clay said, and, going outside, climbed the stairs to Land's office.

He found Land sitting at his desk, Doc Spears across from him. The lawyer's battered nose was bandaged, one eye was shut, and his mouth was so bruised and swollen that it was an effort to talk. When he saw Clay, he shouted: "Get to hell out of here!"

The words were slurred so that they were hard to understand. "You don't talk very plain." Clay closed the door behind him and nodded at Spears. "You're the one I want to see. If I was looking for a lawyer, I wouldn't hire one who was inexperienced like Bill, especially with his face marked up like that."

Land muttered a curse and yanked open his top

drawer. Spears said sharply: "Don't be a fool, Bill."

"That's right," Clay said. "You try using that gun on me again and I'll kill you. I'm not sitting on the walk knocked silly by a sneak punch like I was a while ago."

Land hesitated, his good eye glittering with virulent hatred, then he slammed the drawer shut, and sat back. He said thickly: "Get out."

"What's the matter with you, Bill?" Clay asked. "The whole mesa has gone crazy, and I'd say you're the craziest one on the mesa unless it's Queen Bess. All the time I was riding back, I was figuring you were the one man I could count on. Well, I sure figured wrong."

"I represent Missus Flagg," Land said. "It is my duty to inform you that the Bar C has been absorbed by the Flagg Ranch and you will be treated as an outlaw if you attempt to operate it as a ranch."

Clay cuffed his hat back, staring at Land and shaking his head. "Sounds like you've been reading Queen Bess's special set of law books. Maybe she can steal my range, but she sure as hell can't take a quarter-section of deeded land. Even a stupid lawyer knows better than that."

"You're forgetting you're on Skull Mesa," Doc Spears said. "You're right when you talk about Queen Bess's special set of law books. They're the ones we go by here."

Land motioned to the door, a quick, violent gesture. "Get out. By God, I won't tell you again."

Clay didn't move. He kept his gaze on the lawyer, wondering if this was the same Bill Land he used to ride with. He asked: "How's Rusty?"

"I don't know," Land answered. "He never comes to town any more."

"He has to keep off the mesa, doesn't he?" Clay pressed. "That's more of Queen Bess's law, isn't it?"

Land got up, his fists clenched in front of him. "It's not like it was six years ago, Clay. Can't you understand that? Can't you savvy that if you stay here, you're committing suicide?"

"No, it isn't the same for a fact," Clay said. "We used to have a lot of fun, you and me and Rusty, but it looks like we never will again."

"We were boys, then," Land said. "Just kids, helling around. You think you can ride off and come back six years later and find that life has stood still all the time you were gone? You think you can pick up with Linda just like those six years were six days?"

"No, I couldn't expect that," Clay admitted, and yet he knew that was just about what he had expected. "But I sure didn't think I'd find you bought and paid for by Queen Bess." Clay turned to Spears. "He's no different than everyone else on the mesa, is he, Doc?"

"No one except old man Cryder," Spears said, "and he's starving to death. Anybody who bucks Queen Bess will starve to death." He grinned mockingly. "What did you expect to gain, coming up here and talking tough as hell to us?"

Spears was a small, weasel-faced man in his middle thirties. He had not been considered a good doctor six years ago, but he was the only one within fifty miles. It was probably the same now. Like Bill Land, he wanted to be on the winning side. Maybe what he had said was true, that you starved to death if you weren't on that side.

"I came here to ask a question," Clay said. "Was my father kicked to death by a horse or was he murdered?"

"No question about it," Spears said blandly. "He was kicked to death by a horse."

"I think you're lying," Clay said. "I expect to see you again one of these days, and when I do, I'll get a different answer out of you."

"I'll see you, but you won't see me," Spears said. "I'm an undertaker, too, you know."

Clay wheeled and left Land's office. He would get the same answer everywhere he went, but now that he had gone this far, he'd go a little farther, for the record if nothing else.

Crossing the street to the barbershop, he found Ed Parker alone. Clay said: "I want to ask you a question, Ed."

Parker wasn't wearing a gun, but the marshal's star was on his vest. He glanced at the star as if he thought it held some magic that would give him strength. Finding none, he backed up so he stood behind his chair. "I'm not wearing a gun, Clay."

"Do you need one?"

"I don't know. I don't know why you're here."

"Funny thing, Ed. I used to have a lot of friends in this town. I've sat in that chair a hundred times and we talked about a lot of things. It was the same when I'd go into the Belle Union. Or just stand on the street. Hunting talk. Fishing talk. Cow talk. The kind that goes on between friends, but do you know that in the hour or so I've been in town only one man has offered to shake hands with me?"

"You know the reason." Parker shook his head sadly. "Every day I think about moving with my wife and children, but I stay. We've been here a long time and I keep thinking that something will happen to change the situation, but it never does and I guess it never will."

He was honest, Clay thought, more honest than Bill Land or Doc Spears. He was big and strong, with unusually supple fingers for a man of his size. Clay had never seen him draw a gun, but he might be reasonably fast. It wouldn't help if he was, for there was no real courage in him. Most of the townsmen were like Parker, Clay told himself, probably the mesa ranchers were, too. The only man on the mesa who had any sand in his craw was Anton Cryder, and, as he said, he was too old and sick to fight.

"I feel sorry for you, Ed," Clay said. "You don't sleep very well, do you?"

"No, I haven't slept very well since Queen Bess hired Abe Lavine and Pete Reno." Parker motioned toward the Belle Union. "Five men have been shot to death over there in less'n a year. I saw it happen twice. The other three times I was sent for after it was over. All five times I had to call it justifiable homicide. Self-defense. They weren't even held for trial."

"Were all these killings in fair fights?"

"Sure, if you want to call 'em that, but Lavine and Reno are gunslicks. They were brought here to put the fear of the Lord into the rest of us and they have. I wouldn't have any chance against either one of 'em. No more'n I would against you. Neither would Bill Land nor Doc Spears or Bud Walters." He hesitated, then added in a belittling tone: "Somebody's got to wear the star. Once in a while I lock up a drunk. That's all I'm good for."

"How would it work if I wore that star for a while," Clay said. "I wouldn't want the job permanent. I'd see you got it back."

"The town wouldn't hire you," Parker said.

"Because Queen Bess wants me to move on,

I suppose," Clay said. "Anton Cryder gave me two or three reasons to stay. One was that a lot of people hate her. If I stayed, I might turn out to be a leader for those people. You won't admit it, but for the sake of your family you'd like to see things different. For the right to sleep at night, too, I guess. Could be that there are a lot of other people like you."

Parker shook his head. "It's no use, Clay. Get off the mesa while you can. They'll kill you if you stay. I've heard it said too many times after your pa was killed."

"I've handled men like Lavine and Reno," Clay said. "I can do it here."

"They're just symptoms, boy," Parker said wearily. "They're not the cause. Suppose you did kill 'em? She'd hire others."

Clay nodded, knowing it was true. "All right, Ed. I came in to ask you if you knew anything about Dad's killing. Or Long Sam Kline's. I heard both men were murdered."

"I don't know nothing about 'em," Parker said. "I don't have any authority outside of town. You know that."

"And if you knew, you wouldn't tell me, would you?" Clay said bitterly.

He walked out of the barbershop, not waiting for Parker's answer. As he strode along the walk toward his horse tied in front of the Mercantile, he thought about going in and asking Bud Walters if he could have credit to buy supplies to last the winter. But it wouldn't do any good. Walters would be like the rest. He'd tell Clay he wasn't a good risk. Queen Bess knew all the ways to squeeze a man, and credit or lack of it was one of the best. She had the town treed and no mistake.

He untied his horse and, mounting, rode out of Painted Rock. Everyone would be relieved when they saw him go, he thought. They'd be more relieved if he left the mesa, but that was something they'd never see.

Now that Clay had read his father's letter, he knew he could live on the Bar C alone. Maybe it wouldn't make any sense to anyone else, but it did to him. For the first time in six years he was at peace with the memory of his father. The letter had done that for him.

Suddenly the thought struck him that Ed Parker had been right about symptoms. On an impulse he turned off the road and angled north toward the Flagg Ranch. He had always believed that the way to head off trouble was to meet it before it got to him. Trouble with the Flagg outfit was too certain and too big to head off, but at least he'd show Bess he wasn't running. He might be foolish to take the risk, but he had little to lose and he might gain something. At least it made more sense than arguing with men like Bill Land and Doc Spears.

Chapter Nine

Linda was kneeling on one side of Bill Land, Doc Spears on the other, when Abe Lavine took her firmly by the arm and pulled her to her feet. He half led and half dragged her down the street to the buggy.

"I'm going to take you home," Lavine said. "You can't do him any good."

She knew he was right. He gave her a hand into the buggy seat, then untied the horse and stepped up beside her. Taking the lines, he drove out of town.

She sat huddled there, her hands folded on her lap, shoulders hunched forward, not feeling the chill wind that blew across the mesa. She hated Bill Land. Still, she knew she had been wrong. She shouldn't have come to town. She shouldn't have called to Clay. She shouldn't have let him kiss her.

Linda was not always honest with other people, but she was with herself. She had come to town in hopes of seeing Clay; she would have been miserable if she hadn't called to him, and she had enjoyed his kiss. In that one sweet moment she had been stirred in a way that no man had stirred her since Clay had left.

Staring at the dusty ribbon of road stretching

ahead of the buggy like a taut, gray ribbon, she asked herself why she had ever promised to marry Bill Land. She didn't love him. She never had, she never would, and she had never told him she did. He said he loved her, but she didn't believe it. It would be a marriage of convenience for both of them—security for her, and for him a capable wife who would be a credit to him and his career.

After Clay had left, she'd turned down several men who would have made acceptable husbands. She should have left the country with Clay when he asked her, but her mother had been alive then and her mother had needed her. Besides, the desire for security had always been strong in her mind, and security was one thing Clay could not give her. Still, the hope that someday Clay would come back for her had been the reason she had turned down the men who had courted her. She was well on the road toward becoming an old maid when her mother died and Queen Bess gave her a job.

Linda had been reasonably happy with Queen Bess and that was a strange thing. Bess had no friends unless you call men like Riley Quinn and Bill Land friends. She had been terribly lonely, so she had hired Linda, a paid companion who would sit with her and sew or read or talk if Bess felt like talking. No real work was required except helping Bess dress or take a bath or get into bed.

The strangest part of the arrangement was that Bess had made it plain from the beginning that she wanted Linda to marry Bill Land. He began courting her from the time she had moved out to the Flagg Ranch and Bess had said repeatedly that Bill had a great future ahead of him, in politics as well as law. She was going to have him run for the legislature next year.

As Mrs. William Land, Linda would have all the security in the world, so she had finally surrendered and accepted his ring, but that had been a year ago. Somehow she had succeeded in putting off the wedding date, much to Land's disappointment. She couldn't do it much longer. Both Bess and Land were getting impatient.

After what had happened today . . . She was sick with fear as she thought about it. She'd lose her job. Bess would have a tantrum if she found out Clay had kissed her and then beaten Bill Land into the dust the way he had. She could not stand defeat and Bill Land's defeat was hers.

They were a mile from town when Lavine's words broke into her thoughts: "Damn a man who hits a woman. You can't marry him. You're too good for him."

She looked at him in surprise. He was not one to let his feelings show in either his voice or his face, but now he spoke in hot anger. She saw it in the somber cast of his strong-featured face, heard it in the harsh tone of his voice.

Impulsively she laid a hand on his arm. "Thank you," she said, "but I'm not good. It's the wrong word to use about me."

"No it isn't," he said quickly. "You're a woman a man should be proud to call his wife. You're not a woman to be batted around on the street in front of everybody."

"I don't know," she said miserably. "I was wrong, but he was more wrong. It was just that I hadn't seen Clay for so long . . ." She stopped, unable to tell him how wrong she had been, how much she had wanted to see Clay, and what his kiss had done to her. She added: "Bess will have a fit when she hears."

"You don't have to stay out there," he said. "Quit your job and give Land's ring back to him. You're not a slave to be sold or bought." When she remained silent, he demanded: "You're not in love with Land, are you?"

"No, I'm not," she said, and wondered why she was admitting it to Lavine. She tried to change the subject. "Did you get the posters?"

"No, they won't be ready till evening." He gave her a searching look, then he said bluntly: "You can't love Clay Roland, either. You can't love a man who went off and left you for six years, a man who will be dead in a matter of hours."

That shocked her. She knew it, but still it was shocking to hear it said so bluntly. Her hand tightened on his arm. "Abe . . . ," she said, and

90

stopped, realizing it was the first time she had ever called him by his first name. She hurried on. "Can't you help him? It isn't fair for him to come back and have his home taken away from him and get killed because Bess wants his land or just hates him because she hated his father."

"No, it isn't fair," Lavine admitted, "but there isn't much that goes on around here that is fair. There won't be as long as Queen Bess runs things. I've known a lot of cattle barons. Men, I mean. They all run to about the same pattern. The bigger they get, the bigger they want to be, squeezing and strangling everybody who's in their way.

"Most of my jobs have been helping men like that. I've always hated them because they didn't have enough courage to do the job they hired me to do. Bess is the worst I ever ran into, her and Riley Quinn. Now it seems like I can't stand myself any more. I guess it's partly because I like the cut of Clay Roland's jib. Like you say, it isn't fair, though I never thought much about fairness before. But there's nothing I can do for him."

He pulled the horse to a stop and turned to her. "Linda, I said to myself a while ago when we were going to town that I wouldn't tell you how I felt about you. I'm too old for you and I've got too many men on my back trail who will try to kill me if they ever catch up with me, but after what happened in town, I've got to tell you. I love you. I want you to marry me. Today. Tomorrow. As soon as you can. Then I'll take you away from here."

She stared at him, wide-eyed. She had never been more surprised in her life. She had talked to Lavine so few times; she had never dreamed he had any decent human emotions. He was a cold-blooded killing machine, or so she had thought, but now she sensed a softness in him she hadn't known he possessed.

"Oh, Abe, you never . . . I mean . . ."

She could not say what was in her mind. She could not find the right words, but he seemed to understand. "I know how people look at me and think about me. Most of them hate me. If you hate me for what I've been and what I've done and what I'll probably have to do in the future, say so and that will be the end of it. I'll never speak to you about it again."

"I don't hate you," she said. "It's just that I never thought of you that way, but I know I've got to leave here and maybe you're the one to take me. I need to think about it. I've got to think about Clay, too. It was a shock, seeing him today."

"I'll wait," he said. "You think about it."

She leaned forward, her face close to his. Slowly she raised her hands to the sides of his face and kissed him, then she sat back, smiling at him. "I don't understand this. I never knew you before, but all of a sudden it seems that I do."

Embarrassed, he spoke to the horse and they went on. Presently he said: "No one knows me, Linda. I've never let anyone know me, but I want you to. Maybe in time you will love me. I've loved you ever since I've been here. I like to watch you, the way you move, the way your face changes expression with your feelings."

He had been staring straight ahead, but now he looked at her again. "You don't belong here, Linda. Not with Bess Flagg. If you stay long enough, you'll be warped and twisted into something different than what you are now. I've got to get you out of here before that happens."

She nodded, knowing what he meant. At times the feeling of evil about the Flagg place was so great that it stifled her. This had been more noticeable since Bess's accident. Yet, surprisingly enough, Bess was usually a pleasant person to work for. She would sit at her desk for hours, working on her books, sometimes humming a tune that was running through her mind, or she'd sit on the front porch, her binoculars to her eyes as she studied the movements on the grass. She demanded very little of Linda except her company.

Linda could remember only one occasion when Bess had been angry with her. That was after Linda had heard about John Roland's death and she had said she hoped Clay returned to live on the Bar C. Bess had lit into her as if she'd said something treasonable, then she'd looked straight at Linda and said: "He'll never live on the Bar C or anywhere else on this mesa if I have to kill him."

There had been times when she had seen Bess furious with her housekeeper, Ellie, or some of the crew, so furious she had seemed almost crazy. Linda wasn't sure why, with that one exception, she had been spared the bite of the woman's anger unless it was that Bess felt the need for company, and she knew Linda would be hard to replace.

Lavine spoke only once more before they reached the Flagg house. "I guess I've known all the time that the day would come when I'd hang up my guns. It's here. Or will be when you make up your mind. There is one thing you should know before you decide. I have a little over ten thousand dollars in a Denver bank. If you go with me, we'll take it and buy a business somewhere a long ways from here. California. Oregon. Anywhere you say."

She smiled at him, thinking that $10,000 was a fortune and that she would not have many more opportunities to marry a man with that much money. Probably none. This was heady wine, the knowledge that a man like Lavine loved her, that he was thinking of her future as well as his.

The need for security was always in her

mind, some insurance against having to marry a poverty-stricken rancher or keeping house for one. At this moment, tormented as she was with the knowledge that she had to break with Bill Land and that Clay could promise her nothing, the thought of marrying a man who was worth $10,000 was dazzling.

"I think I'd like California," she murmured. "I've heard so much about the nice climate."

She hooked her arm through his and sat close to him so that he would feel the pressure of her breast. Her mind was made up now, but she wouldn't tell him yet. It was better to let a man dangle for a while. A woman who came too easily was a cheap thing. She could not afford to have Lavine think of her that way.

He did not stop in front of the house, but drove on past it to the corral. Bess was sitting on the porch, watching them, and suddenly Linda was uneasy as she wondered how she was going to tell Bess about what had happened in town.

Pete Reno had been lounging in the bunkhouse doorway. Now he strolled across the yard, a cigarette dangling from his mouth. Lavine swung down from the seat and wrapped the lines around the brake handle, then gave Linda a hand as she stepped to the ground.

"Any excitement in town?" Reno asked.

"A little," Lavine said. "Clay Roland showed up."

"You kill him?"

"No. Put this horse away."

"What the hell!" Reno said, backing up. "I ain't no hostler."

Lavine stepped away from Linda. He said quietly: "Put up the horse, Pete."

Reno swallowed and turned his gaze away. "Sure, Abe."

Linda had started toward the house. Lavine caught up with her, saying: "Let me do the talking."

Linda said in a low tone: "How can you stand him, Abe? I feel dirty just having him look at me."

"I'm not going to stand him much longer," Lavine said. "I saved his life two years ago. I thought I could do something for him, but I can't." He paused, the small smile touching the corners of his lips again. "Once in a while I get a sentimental notion that surprises me. I thought I was responsible for Pete because I saved his life, but that's crazy thinking. When I ride out of here, he's not riding with me."

"He'll get himself killed in a year," Linda said.

"In a month," Lavine corrected her. "If I couldn't learn him anything in two years, I couldn't do any better in ten."

When they reached the porch, Bess asked: "Get the posters?"

"No," Lavine said. "They won't be ready till evening. Clay Roland was in town. He saw

Linda and kissed her, and Bill Land hit him. Then Roland beat hell out of Land. I didn't want to leave Linda in town after that. I'll pick up the posters in the morning."

"Why didn't you shoot him?" Bess demanded. "You know I want that bastard dead."

"It was Bill Land's fight," Lavine said. "Missus Flagg, there are times when you think like a man, but there are other times when you just don't understand. If Bill Land is going to be anything more than your legal puppy, he's got to finish anything he starts."

Bess flushed with the criticism, and for a moment Linda thought that the woman's temper was going to boil up again, but there was too much truth in what Lavine said for her to ignore it. Besides, Lavine had a way of saying things like that to Bess and making her take it, a quality that Linda had not seen in any other man.

"All right." Bess jerked her hand at the bunkhouse. "I'll send for you if I want you."

"Yes, ma'am," Lavine said.

He touched the brim of his hat and strode away. Linda watched him go, wanting to cry out for him to take her away now, that to go on the way they had been was a dangerous thing for both of them, but she couldn't bring herself to say it. Then she heard Bess's harsh voice: "Will you explain to me why you let a man like Clay Roland kiss you?"

Linda looked at Bess. She saw the way the

older woman's face had turned ugly, the way her lips were pulled tightly against her teeth. These were familiar storm signals Linda had seen too many times.

"I was in the store when I saw him walk by," Linda said slowly, knowing that the choosing of each word was important. "I called to him. When he saw me, he grabbed me and lifted me off my feet and whirled me around. Then he kissed me."

"And just what were you doing all that time?"

"What could I do?" Linda demanded. "I was in his arms. He's a big man."

"Yes, I suppose he is." Bess eased back in her chair, her anger fading. "Bill saw it and didn't like it? That it?"

"No, he sure didn't," Linda admitted.

"I don't blame him," Bess said. "I don't blame him one bit. Well, go get your fancy work and sit a while."

Linda fled into the house, glad to get out of it that easily. She hadn't told Bess the whole story. There would be trouble later when Bess heard it, and sooner or later Bill Land would ride out here and tell it. She ran upstairs to her room. She didn't go back for a time, but she couldn't dawdle all afternoon. When she had taken as much time as she dared, she picked up her sewing basket and went back down the stairs.

When she reached the porch, Bess said: "Get my shawl. It's a little chilly."

Linda went back into Bess's room and returned with a red shawl. She wrapped it around Bess's shoulders, and sat down in a rocking chair. She was embroidering a table runner, busy work that she enjoyed. For a time she sat in silence, her mind on Lavine. She would make him a good wife, she told herself. It seemed a miracle, a man like that telling her he loved her, a miracle lifting her out of a situation that had become more difficult with each passing day. She couldn't keep on postponing her wedding and she had not been able to think of any way out of her bargain.

Bess had been watching the road through her glasses. Linda saw a rider coming in across the grass, but she didn't recognize him. Bess put the binoculars on her lap, swearing softly. She always kept a small revolver in her chair beside her. Now she laid it across her lap and, pulling the shawl from her shoulders, dropped it over the revolver.

"Get Lavine," Bess said. "Have him keep Reno in the bunkhouse in case we need him."

Alarmed, Linda put her sewing on the floor beside her chair. "What's the matter?"

"Matter?" Bess said angrily. "There's plenty the matter. That's Clay Roland coming. He's either a fool or a brave man. Now get a move on."

Linda did. As she raced across the yard to the bunkhouse, she thought dismally that this was the worst thing that could happen.

Chapter Ten

After Clay left the road and turned toward the Flagg Ranch, he thought about Queen Bess and what he would say to her. He had never been well acquainted with her, although he used to see her in town on Saturdays and on a few occasions had been in her house.

He had worked roundup with her crew along with the other small ranchers on the mesa. He had seen her a few times when she visited the roundup camp, although he doubted that she had been aware of his presence. Usually she talked to her foreman, Riley Quinn, and ignored everyone else. When she visited the Bar C, it was on Sunday afternoon when Clay had a date with Linda or a ride rigged with Rusty Mattson and Bill Land.

The more he thought about it, the more the present situation seemed incredible. But the most incredible part was Anton Cryder's statement that she had been in love with Clay's father and that her hatred for Clay stemmed from that frustrated love. Still, he could not overlook a few facts. Cryder wouldn't lie. His father would have confided in Cryder as he would in no other man because Cryder had been his only close friend. What the lawyer had said, then, must be true.

The Flagg buildings loomed ahead of Clay—the sprawling house, the barns and corrals and bunkhouse and various outbuildings. No change here at all. In fact, there had been few if any changes since Hank Flagg had died. He had built big and he had built well, utility his only object except with the house that had been built for show.

The point that used to strike Clay and still did was the complete absence of feminine touches—no trees around the house, no flowers, no curtains at the windows. A stranger riding in would have thought this was a bachelor's ranch.

Clay approached the house slowly, not at all sure he had been smart in obeying the impulse that had brought him here. Bess Flagg was in her wheelchair on the front porch, Linda sitting on one side of her, Abe Lavine standing on the other.

Clay's gaze swept the yard. A man stood in the bunkhouse door. He was a stranger. He must, Clay thought, be the Pete Reno that Ardis Kline had mentioned. He wouldn't be here in the middle of the afternoon if he were a member of the crew.

Reining up in front of the porch, Clay touched the brim of his hat as he said: "Howdy, Missus Flagg. Howdy, Linda." He nodded at Lavine who nodded back, his lean, strong-featured face expressionless. Linda was plainly frightened, but Clay couldn't tell what was in Bess Flagg's mind.

She looked older than he remembered her, older than the additional six years should have made her. Aside from that, she had changed very little and that surprised Clay. For an active woman to be imprisoned in a wheelchair must be little short of hell.

"I was sorry to hear about your accident, Missus Flagg," Clay said.

"You didn't come here to tell me that, Roland," Bess said. "State your business."

She made no effort to keep the hostility out of her voice, but that, Clay told himself, was exactly what he had expected. He looked at Lavine. "There's a man standing in the bunkhouse door. If he's been put there to shoot me, I want to know it."

"That's up to you," Lavine said. "He won't throw any lead if you don't start the ball."

"I didn't come for that." Clay brought his gaze back to Bess Flagg. He wished Linda wasn't here. He didn't want to see her, even to think about her and Bill Land. "Missus Flagg, I was told by Anton Cryder today that you had made an offer for the Bar C. I rode out here to tell you I'm not selling. I plan to live there."

"No, you won't live there," she snapped. "When your father was alive, I let the Bar C alone because he was an old friend, but I owe you nothing. If you think I'm going to let a two-bit outfit like the Bar C exist in the middle of my range, you're crazy. You'd better take what you can get for it and move on."

Clay sat quite still, watching the man in the bunkhouse without appearing to do so. He could take him, or he could take Lavine, but he couldn't take both if they went for their guns at the same time. After what Lavine had said, Clay didn't think they would, but if Reno was the jumpy kind, he might start it. If he did, Lavine wouldn't stand still.

"This is downright peculiar, Missus Flagg," Clay said. "You don't need the Bar C, but ever since I've got back, people have been telling me you're going to drive me out of the country."

"That's right," she said, "so don't be a fool and try to hang on."

"I would be a worse fool if I walked off and left it," he said. "I never like to believe gossip, but I've heard quite a bit since I got back. That's the real reason I rode out here. I know where you stand. Now you know where I stand, but there is one thing I still don't savvy. That's the why of it."

"I told you," she said in her harsh voice. "If you have a pimple on your face, you pop it out. You don't let it get bigger and bigger. The Bar C is a pimple on the face of Flagg range."

"I have no intention of making the Bar C bigger," he said. "It's no threat to you. Neither am I. All I'm asking is the right to live on my property. Is that too much to ask?"

"Way too much," she said. "This is the time to close the Bar C out and that's exactly what I aim to do. Now get to hell out of here before I lose my temper."

"Not yet," he said. "Cryder told me you were in love with my father, but he wouldn't have you, so you hated him. Is that why you hate me?"

"It's a god-damned lie!" she screamed. "Shoot him, Lavine! Cut him out of the saddle. I won't be insulted. . . ."

"Is that the reason you had Dad murdered?" Clay broke in.

Her face went dead white. For a brief moment she sat, motionless, her lips parted, then she cried out, an incoherent sound, and throwing the shawl to one side, snatched the gun from her lap.

"No, Bess!" Linda screamed, and grabbed her arm.

Clay made no move, knowing that the slightest motion on his part would bring the man out of the bunkhouse, his gun smoking. He heard Bess Flagg curse him as if she were a crazy woman while she struggled with Linda, then Lavine reached down and took the gun from her.

"You've said enough, Roland," Lavine said. "You'd better ride."

"I hoped it wouldn't be like this," Clay said. "I wasn't sure before that Dad was murdered, but I am now. That's more than enough reason for me to stay on this range."

He rode away, turning his head to watch the man in the bunkhouse doorway until he was out of revolver range. If Riley Quinn and the crew had been here, he wouldn't have left without a fight. He would probably have been shot out of his saddle. Lavine, for reasons of his own, had not made a fight of it, and he had probably called the turn for Pete Reno. Tomorrow would be another day. Even tonight . . . He shook his head. There was simply no way of telling what Bess Flagg would do.

Clay had often been successful in putting himself in another man's place and figuring out what he would do, but he could not put himself in Bess Flagg's place. Six years ago he had considered her a rational woman, running her spread in a business-like way as a man would have done. When he had first seen her, he thought she hadn't changed except for the lines that time had carved in her face, but now he knew he had been wrong.

Bess Flagg was nothing like the woman he had known six years before. She was crazy. When he had told her what Cryder had said, Clay had seen her face change. The only way he could describe it was that she had suddenly lost her reason. Then he realized that maybe she hadn't changed at all, that he had never seen her goaded into the wild fury that he had brought on. Now he knew exactly where he stood.

Perhaps he would never know the whole truth about her and his father. He might never know how his father had died, but he hadn't wasted his time riding to the Flagg Ranch. He had brought the trouble to a head. If a fight was inevitable, he wanted it to come soon. He had no capacity for waiting.

When he reached the Bar C, he watered and fed his horse. He went into the house and walked through the empty rooms again as he had early that morning, pausing at the chessboard and thinking how it was with Anton Cryder.

Cryder was a lonely old man, his legal business destroyed, his one good friend killed. Now he might feel the knife of Bess Flagg's anger. Clay regretted that. He thought about riding back to town and asking Cryder to move out here, but that would be foolish, for the Bar C was the most dangerous place on the mesa.

On more than one occasion Clay had arrested men for murder. He had attended the trials, he had seen their faces when the judge sentenced them to death, and he had watched them slowly wither and die while they waited for their date with the rope. In a way he was in the same position. Bess Flagg had decreed his execution. There was nothing for him to do but wait.

Chapter Eleven

To Linda each passing second was an eternity while Clay rode away. She wasn't sure what Lavine would do and she was even less sure about Pete Reno. She dropped a hand on Bess's shoulder. She had the disturbing feeling that the woman had been turned to stone. Suddenly Bess began to tremble. She raised her right hand and, gripping Linda's wrist, flung her arm away. She glanced at Linda, the corners of her mouth working, then she looked at Lavine.

"I sure hired me a pair of dandies," she said bitterly. "By God, I did."

Clay was out of range of her gun now. Lavine laid it in her lap. He said: "You're mixed up, Missus Flagg. You don't recognize loyalty when you see it."

"Loyalty?" She glared at him. "Now that's a damned funny word for you to use. You knew I wanted that bastard dead, but you didn't have the guts to do the job. I would have, but you wouldn't let me. You call that loyalty?"

"Yes, ma'am," Lavine said.

"Oh, hell." Bess glared at Linda who had sat down in her chair. "You used to be sweet on him. Maybe you still are. That the reason you grabbed my arm?"

Linda picked up the embroidery she had dropped. "No, Bess," she said. "He came out here in good faith to talk to you. If you had shot him, it would have been murder. He wouldn't shoot at a woman. I think you knew that."

"Sure I did." Bess turned her head to glare at Lavine. "You aren't in love with him. What's your excuse?"

"I don't have any excuse," he said. "I kept you from making a serious mistake."

She threw up her arms in disgust. "You heard him say what he was going to do and you know I'm taking the Bar C. He's not like the sheep we've been dealing with. What else is there to do but kill him?"

"In the right place and time," he said. "I can't seem to make you understand that, Missus Flagg. I've been here long enough to know how some of these people feel that you call sheep. You've got them buffaloed now, all right, but I've seen sheep become wolves. It could happen on this mesa if you kill Clay Roland under circumstances like you were going to."

"Lavine, I don't know how in hell you could have got the reputation you have," Bess said hotly. "You talk like a cautious old woman."

"I am cautious," he admitted. "A man in my profession has to be or he doesn't live long. In time I'll get the job done without any risk to you. In the year Pete and me have worked for you, we've rubbed out five men. Men you wanted out of the way. I got two because they accused me of cheating in a poker game. The other one was because I overheard him making a remark about you. Pete got his because he heard 'em cussing the Flagg outfit and some of Riley Quinn's deals. People don't like us because of those killings, but they were fair fights and Ed Parker had nothing to hold us on. You didn't get any blame except for hiring us."

"And I suppose you think you'll get into a poker game with Roland? Or you'll hear him making an insulting remark about me?"

"Something of the kind," Lavine said. "But when you let Quinn do a job like he did on Long Sam Kline and John Roland, you're taking a chance on turning every man on the mesa against you."

"How do you know Quinn killed them?" she demanded.

"I added it up," he said. "It's a simple matter of two and two making four. If I can add it up and get the answer, so can other men. It didn't take Clay Roland long. I've learned one thing in this business, Missus Flagg. If you've got to kill a man, do it in the open where men can see it done and know why. Both of those killings were mistakes and I'd have told you so if I'd had a chance."

"I believe you would have," she said slowly.

109

"You tell me more things I don't want to hear than anyone else on the mesa. Someday I'm going to fire you because of it."

"But not until my usefulness to you is gone," he said. "I'm not sure I'll stay here that long."

She leaned back, her eyes closed. "I'm tired. Go on back to the bunkhouse. Linda, wheel me inside and call Ellie. I think I'll lie down for a while."

Lavine stepped away from her chair, his gaze meeting Linda's briefly. He said—"Yes, ma'am."—and left the porch.

Linda pushed Bess into her bedroom, then called Ellie from the kitchen, and together they lifted Bess from her chair to the bed. She said: "I won't need you till evening, Linda."

"Thank you," Linda said, and fled to her room.

She tried to read but she found her mind wandering so that the words made no sense to her. She returned to the porch and, sitting down, picked up her embroidery, but she was too restless to work on it. She had to see Clay once more. Bess would be furious if she knew, but maybe she'd never find out.

She ran upstairs and changed to a dark-green riding skirt and a leather jacket. She slipped out of the house, hoping Bess wouldn't hear her. Lavine and Reno were talking at the corral gate. Lavine said something to Reno and the younger man walked across the yard toward the bunkhouse.

Linda was aware that Lavine watched every move she made as she approached him. She had been used to his barren expression so long that she had supposed it was a natural part of him, but now she realized that it was a mask to keep people from reading his thoughts. The knowledge came as a surprise to her. She was pleased. She knew a side of him no one else did. Now his lips held a smile that thawed his face. Even his pale blue eyes lost their chill.

When she reached him, he said: "Seems to me you get prettier every day, Linda."

She was pleased by that, too, for complimentary words coming from him were unexpected. She would have a good life with him, she thought, and she would be a foolish woman to turn him down.

"Thank you," she said softly. "It's funny, Abe. I feel that I have made a discovery that no one else has ever made."

"What discovery?"

"There are two Abe Lavines," she answered, smiling. "I'm the only person in the world who knows the real one."

"I hope you do," he said.

He took her into his arms and pulled her to him. He kissed her, tentatively at first, then he did a thorough job. When he released her, she stood close to him, her eyes wide. "Abe, Abe," she breathed. "What are you trying to do to me?"

"Tell you I love you," he said. "I've waited too long. I've got to get you away from here. I saw that this afternoon when Clay Roland was here."

"What do you mean by that?"

"Bess is going to raise hell and prop it up with a stick," he said. "I haven't told Bess this, but the boys out in the Smoky Hills are the ones she'd better watch out for. They're a tough lot and they've been sore ever since Kline died. If she kills Roland, and she's bound to do it, Rusty Mattson will get that bunch together and she'll have the fight of her life."

Linda nodded, thinking about Rusty. She had not seen him for a long time, but before Clay had left the country, she had known Rusty well and she had liked him. He was a red-headed banty of a man, a natural maverick who set himself against all authority. He didn't know what fear was, and he had a fierce loyalty to Clay that was almost unreasonable. At least that was the way he used to be. She didn't think that he had changed.

"Rusty would help Clay if he knew he was back," she said.

"Trouble is he's hard to get hold of. He's on the move all the time." Lavine took her by the shoulders. "Have you decided yet? About me?"

She wanted to tell him that she had, but she must not forget the feminine principle of playing hard to get. "I like you," she said. "I like you more than I ever thought possible, but I've got to get used to the idea."

"I should have told you before," he said with regret, "but you were wearing Land's ring and I never thought you could see anything in a man like me."

"Well, I do," she said, "and I like what I see, but I want my marriage to last as long as I live. You want me to be sure, Abe. I know you do."

"Yes," he said. "I sure do. I wouldn't be hurrying you if all this crazy business wasn't working the way it is. I've got a hunch that neither one of us has much time."

"I know," she said, thinking how Bess had tried to kill Clay. "I want to take a ride, Abe. Maybe I can get my thinking straight if I can get away from here and be alone for a while."

"I'll saddle your mare for you," he said.

She waited beside the gate until he led her mare out of the corral. She rode often, the one relaxation that she'd had since coming here, and she was sure no one would think anything about it today. Lavine gave her a hand into the saddle, then she said: "I never knew how bad Bess was until she tried to shoot Clay. I'd never seen that side of her."

"She's bad enough, and she'll get worse." Lavine stepped back, adding: "Don't stay too long. Too much can happen, the way things are stacking up."

"I'll be all right," she said, and smiled at him before she reined her mare around and left the yard at a gallop.

She took the road to town, pulling the mare down to a slower pace. As soon as she was out of sight of the ranch, she angled westward toward the Bar C. Even Lavine would not understand why she had to see Clay, she thought. She wasn't sure herself, actually, except that she wanted to see him again, to talk to him, perhaps to bury an old love that had never really died.

As she rode, her thoughts turned to Lavine. She didn't love him. She never would, but she would tell him she did. He would never regret his bargain with her. She did not doubt his statement that he had more than $10,000 in the bank. She could afford to lie a little to a man who had that much money. Perhaps, with his record, he would never be able to put up his guns. She might be a widow within weeks or months, but that wouldn't be so bad. She'd have the $10,000.

She found Clay building a fire in his kitchen range when she reached the Bar C. He hadn't seen her ride up, so, when she appeared in the kitchen doorway, he stared at her as if he thought he was dreaming and she wasn't real.

"Clay," she said. "I thought you'd be glad to see me."

"I'm glad to see you," he said, "but I've dreamed about you too many times in the years

I've been gone to believe it's really you. You're just another dream."

"I'm real," she said. "I'll prove it."

She crossed the room to him and kissed him, confident that he still loved her. She stepped back, disappointed and hurt, for he had not returned her kiss. He hadn't even put his arms around her.

"What's the matter, Clay?" she demanded. "You didn't act like this in town."

"I didn't know you were going to marry Bill," he said. "I should have asked if you were married or engaged. I have no claim on you. I couldn't expect you to wait for me when I didn't even write to you."

He swallowed, busying himself with the fire for a moment, then he added: "I guess I can't even blame Bill for being sore. From the way you kissed me, I sure didn't figure any other man had his loop on you." He motioned toward the door. "I guess you'd better go."

"Not yet!" she cried angrily. "I won't let you treat me this way. I'm not going to marry Bill. I don't know why I ever said I would. I don't love him and I never did."

"All right," he said, "you've loved me all this time, but you won't marry me because I'm not any better risk than when I left six years ago. I may be dead by morning." He motioned toward the door again. "You're still wearing Bill's ring. I don't want you here. He tried to kill me in town. If he finds out you came here to see me, he'll have a real excuse to kill me."

She had intended to tell him she was going to marry Lavine, that she would get Lavine to help him and he ought to try to find Rusty Mattson, but she was too furious to tell him anything.

"I think you will be dead by morning," she cried, "and I hope you are!"

She whirled and ran out of the house. She stepped into the saddle, and quirted her mare into a run. She didn't mean what she had said, but she wasn't going back to apologize. He didn't want her help. Well, that was all right because he sure wasn't going to get it. He'd find out how far he'd get bucking Queen Bess by himself.

Chapter Twelve

Dusk was moving in across the mesa by the time Clay finished supper and cleaned up the kitchen. It had been a struggle to force down the food, but he knew he had to do it. He might be on the run by morning and not have another chance to eat for a long time.

After he finished, the food lay like a rock in his stomach. He'd cooked and eaten too many meals by himself, he thought. It was no way to live. He had expected a different life here on the Bar C. In spite of all logic about the matter, he had hoped to find Linda waiting for him; he had hoped to tell her he could support her now that he owned a ranch. He had expected to marry her and bring her here and have the kind of life any normal man wanted.

It was fine and dandy to tell himself that this was the idle dreaming of a lonely man, that it was only natural for a woman of Linda's age to marry or become engaged. As he had told her, he had no hold upon her, no reason to think she would wait for a man who had not bothered to write to her during the time he had been gone. But the cold fact was he could not be logical about it.

He wouldn't have been hit as hard as he was if she hadn't called to him there in front of the

Mercantile, if she had told him she was engaged, if she hadn't returned his kiss with the passion of a woman who still loved him and had been waiting for him to come back to her.

She must have known Bill Land would see them kissing and that he'd be furious. Clay would have felt the same way if the situation had been reversed. Then to find her out there on the Flagg porch beside Queen Bess—and her coming here and kissing him and telling him she wasn't going to marry Bill Land, after all. It was too much, far too much. Either she had changed or he had never really known her.

No, that was wrong. She hadn't changed and he had known her. He began remembering things about her he had wanted to forget. Time and distance and loneliness had made him idealize her in a foolish, adolescent way. She had been a flirt even when she had been his girl and everyone on the mesa had known she belonged to him.

When he had taken her to dances, he had never been sure how many times he would be able to dance with her. When he had taken her to basket and pie socials, she had often told other boys what her pies and baskets looked like and he had been forced to outbid his rivals and pay twice as much as he should for the privilege of eating with her.

He could think of plenty of things to hold against her, but the worst was her refusal to go away with him. Sure, her mother was an excuse, but the truth was she was afraid to risk the security she had here in Painted Rock, living in her own home among people she knew. But if a woman really loved a man, she would go with him wherever he went and not give the flimsy excuses he had heard six years ago.

He had to quit thinking about her, he told himself. It was time he started figuring out how to survive. That was exactly the problem, survival or death. After his visit to the Flagg Ranch, he had no illusions about the next few days. He'd be hunted as if he were an outlaw.

He filled a flour sack with food, thinking that if he did have to make a run for it, at least he wouldn't starve. In the end the Flagg outfit might get him, but they'd know they'd been in a fight before they did.

He stepped out through the back door and stood motionlessly for a moment, his gaze sweeping the narrow valley and the crest of the ridge to the north. The sun was down now, the sky afire with its passing, the gold and scarlet banners reaching out to the far rim of the earth.

A terrifying prickle ran down his spine as he considered the impossible odds he was facing. Riley Quinn could bring a dozen men if he thought it would take that many, but there was no one Clay Roland could call on for help, no lawman he could go to.

He would accomplish nothing by riding to the county seat and demanding protection from the sheriff. He could guess what had happened. Queen Bess had probably told the sheriff that she would deliver the mesa votes if he let the mesa alone after he was elected. No, Clay Roland stood strictly alone.

He stepped into the kitchen, leaving the back door open. He lit a bracket lamp on the wall and, going into the front room, lit another lamp on the claw-footed table. He went out through the front, leaving that door open, too, so that a long finger of light fell across the trodden dirt of the yard. Again his gaze swept the road and the river and the ridge to the south. No sign of life anywhere. Once more the pressure of the terrible loneliness settled down upon him. He had a crazy feeling he would welcome Abe Lavine or even Riley Quinn.

Carrying the sack of grub, he walked quickly to the corral, saddled his bay gelding, and led him around to the west side of the barn. He tied the sack behind the saddle and returned to the east wall of the building, his Winchester in his hands.

The barn was constructed of logs, solid enough to hole up in and fight off the Flagg bunch when it came. He considered bringing his horse inside the barn, shutting the doors from the inside, and waiting until Quinn came. But that would be suicide. He'd be pinned down. Sooner or later they'd set fire to the barn and they'd shoot him when he fled from it.

No, he'd fight as long as he could here on the outside where he could change position. If the odds against him were so big he didn't have a chance, he'd run and keep running until he could turn and fight with the possibility of winning. If he could get into the Smoky Hills and find Rusty Mattson, they'd lead Quinn and his bunch all over hell's back pasture. Rusty knew the hills as well as most men know their front yard. Sooner or later the Flagg bunch would break up into small bands to hunt for him, and then he'd see to it that they found him.

He squatted along the side of the barn, close to the southeast corner, and waited. Night closed in, the last dull glow of the sunset dying above the Smoky Hills, until the only light was that from the windows in the house and the open doors. He wanted to smoke, but decided against it. He had no way of knowing when they would come. If they did, he hoped they would think he was inside the house. That would give him a chance to smash them before they located him.

So he waited, the minutes piling up into an hour, and then another, slow minutes that tightened his nerves until the waiting was intolerable, but it was his kind of game. As a lawman he had faced situations much like this many times. Necessity had taught him patience he had not possessed six years ago.

He dozed off and woke almost at once, sensing that some vagrant sound had stirred him back to consciousness. Suddenly uneasy, he slipped back along the wall of the barn and stood there, seeing only the vague shape of his horse. He listened for a long moment until he was convinced that no one was there, then he returned to the corner where he had been waiting.

He stood motionlessly, still listening and now hearing sounds from the river to the south. He wasn't sure what they were, maybe only innocent noises of the night—a prowling animal slipping through the brush, a breeze rattling the windows, the whirring of a bird's wings. But again they might have been caused by some of Quinn's men. Maybe the whole crew was out there in the darkness, surrounding him to make sure he could not escape when they moved in on him.

The sound did not come again, but still Clay stood there, finding it hard to breathe, the stony fist of fear driving his stomach against his backbone. As he remembered Riley Quinn, the man did not possess the slightest talent for being sly or sneaky or subtle. He was the kind who met an enemy head-on, overpowering him by sheer animal strength. That was why Clay expected him to ride in with his men, boldly and directly without making any effort to disguise their coming.

Suddenly Clay realized there was one possible error in his thinking. Bess Flagg might send Abe Lavine and Pete Reno to do the job. Lavine was smart. Whatever he did would not be with the overriding strength and possible stupidity that would characterize Riley Quinn's action.

The more Clay thought about it, the more he was inclined to reject this possibility. It simply wasn't Lavine's way, judging from what Clay had heard and seen of him. Lavine would wait for him in town and somehow maneuver him into a gunfight for everyone to see. If Lavine was the faster man, Clay would die, and because Lavine was Queen Bess's man, Ed Parker would say it was a fair fight and he had no grounds on which to hold the killer.

Just as Clay had done many times when he'd carried the star, Lavine would gamble on his gun speed saving his life. It was the only way he could operate, but with Queen Bess in the temper she was, Lavine's method would be too slow. No, Riley Quinn would be the one. Clay was as sure of it as he could be sure of anything that depended upon the imponderables of human nature.

Then he heard them, the faint drum of hoofs off to the north. Clay grinned, his nerves relaxing. This was the way he had thought it would be. He did not feel the fist of fear in his stomach, for now he was sure of the action his enemies were taking. It had been the uncertainty that had bothered him.

They came in fast, swinging to the east so they made a wide half circle of the house before they rode in close. Clay could not see them. The moon wasn't up and an overcast covered the sky so that the star shine was blotted out, but from the sound, Clay judged, there weren't many of them, three or maybe four at the most.

They rode toward the front door from the south, having gone almost to the river before they turned toward the house. They reined up in the fringe of lamplight, Quinn bawling: "Roland, we want to see you!"

Clay eared back the hammer of his Winchester, hoping he would not have to fire until they were in the finger of light that fell through the doorway. Apparently there were only three of them. He identified Quinn by his voice, but the other two were only vague shapes in the thin light.

"Roland, if you don't come out, we'll drag you out with a rope around your neck!" Quinn shouted.

"He ain't a fool," one of the men said. "We'll have to go in after him."

"All right, Ives," Quinn said. "Root him out."

"Not by myself," the cowboy snapped. "I hear he's handy with his iron. You get him, Riley."

"Bellew, ride around to the back door," Quinn ordered, ignoring what Ives had said. "We'll give you one minute, then we'll go in the front. Unless he sneaks out through a window, we've got his hide nailed to the front door."

Clay had hoped to get all three massed in the lamplight in front of the house, but now he knew he couldn't afford to wait. He probably wouldn't have a better chance than he had right now.

Bellew was arguing, then Quinn said loudly: "By God, if you want to work for the Flagg outfit, you'll take my orders."

Clay opened up then, pulling the trigger and levering another shell into the chamber and firing again. He couldn't aim in the darkness, so it was almost blind shooting, but he spread his shots from one side of the riders to the other, laying them in about shoulder high on a horse. He was bound to hit something.

His first shot was a miss, but the second brought a yelp of pain from one of the men. They scattered immediately, taking off toward the river. Clay kept shooting, having nothing to go by except the sound of their movements. Quinn gave out one great bawling curse, then he yelled: "He's yonder by the barn! We'll run him down. He can't see no better'n we can."

One of them fired at Clay, the slug ripping into a log above his head. He slipped back along the wall, dropping his empty Winchester and drawing his revolver. He held his fire, not wanting to give them anything to shoot at. They had scattered out and were coming at him on the run, then the completely unexpected happened. Someone cut loose from the river, flashes of powder flame dancing from the willow thicket.

"There's another one out there!" Ives yelled.

"They've got us in a crossfire!" Bellew shouted. "I'm getting out of here. He hit me once. He ain't gonna get a chance to do it again."

"Come on, damn it!" Quinn raged. "It don't make no difference who's in the willows. He's too far away to do any damage."

But Ives and Bellew had whirled their mounts and were digging in the steel, heading east. Quinn hesitated a moment, then he rode after them, apparently having no desire to do the job alone. Clay emptied his revolver, knowing he was wasting lead, but they were on the run and he hoped he would hurry their flight. He reloaded, still hugging the barn wall as he wondered who had sided him in a fight that had been strictly his own affair.

The fading hoof beats were far to the east now. Quinn and his men wouldn't come back. Clay was certain of that. The wounded man would probably go into town and see Doc Spears. Quinn and Ives would return to the Flagg Ranch and the next time Quinn came, he'd have enough men to do the job. Fighting off three cowboys was one thing, but tackling a dozen or more was quite another. Staying would be suicide.

"Who's out there?" Clay called.

"You all right?"

A woman's voice! For one quick, crazy moment Clay thought it was Linda who had returned to help him fight, but the voice wasn't Linda's. It had to be Ardis Kline. There wasn't anyone else it could be.

"I'm all right," he answered, and ran toward the river.

She met him halfway, throwing her arms around him and hugging him with anxious strength. "Clay, Clay. I knew they'd come tonight, but I didn't know where you'd be or what you'd do. I was afraid you were in the house."

"I knew better than that," he said. "Now will you tell me what you're doing here?"

"I came to help you," she said simply. "You needed someone's help, didn't you?"

He wanted to say no, that he had always taken care of himself and he always could, but that would have been his male pride talking. If Ardis hadn't started firing, Quinn and his men would have kept coming and in the darkness anything could have happened. He might have got one, or two if he was lucky, but the chances were that in the end the three-to-one odds would have been too long against him.

"I guess I did," he admitted, "but I sure never aimed for you to risk your hide for me."

"I know you didn't," she said, "but I've been

crazy with worry ever since you left my place. I sent Monroe after Rusty. He thought he could find him, but it may take all night. Rusty couldn't get here till morning and I was afraid it would be too late then."

"Might have been," Clay said. "Where's your horse?"

"By the river. You aren't going to stay here now, are you, Clay? They'll come back. You know that."

"Sure, I know it. I guess I'd better go somewhere." He turned toward the house, calling back: "I'll blow the lamps out!"

She caught his arm. "Clay, where will you go?"

"Off the mesa," he said. "That's all I'm sure of. If Monroe finds Rusty, I'll stay in the Smoky Hills because he knows all the trails and the places to hide."

"I know the trails and the places to hide as well as Rusty does," she said. "I'll guide you, Clay. I can't let you go like you did before."

He didn't understand this. He stared at her in the darkness, seeing only the pale oval of her face. Her hand still clutched his arm, gripping it hard as if she were afraid he'd leave her if she let go.

"Look, Ardis," he said. "They want to kill me. They'll keep after me until they do or I bust them up so bad that the Flagg crew rides out of the country." He paused, realizing there was no way out for him, no chance ever to live here on the mesa and not be hunted. He added bitterly: "Even if they do pull out, she'll hire more men and she'll keep after me till she gets me."

"I know that," Ardis said. "I've thought about this ever since Pa was killed. I could have got Rusty and Monroe and the rest of the Smoky Hills bunch and we could have made Bess a lot of trouble, but none of them would have killed her. She's got to be killed, Clay. You'd shoot a mad dog, wouldn't you?"

"Yes, but I couldn't shoot Bess Flagg. No man could."

"Then I'll do it if I get a chance," she said. "Right now we've got to get to my place. Maybe Rusty will be there, but whether he is or not, I'm going with you."

"You can't. It's my fight, not yours."

"If it's your fight, it's mine," she said impulsively, then paused as if regretting she had said it. She dropped her hand to her side and stepped back. "I mean, it's my fight until the men who killed Pa are punished. Bess, too. She's just as guilty as the men who did it."

He saw no sense in arguing with her now. He said: "Get your horse. I'll be back in a couple of minutes."

He strode toward the house, thinking that

her presence here didn't make any sense. Her insistence that she was going with him made even less. He walked through the house to the kitchen and stood, looking around the familiar room, almost unchanged from the time he had been a boy. Probably he would never see it again. He did not doubt that if he left the Bar C, Bess would burn him out. Suddenly he rebelled against leaving, but the rebellion died almost at once. If he was going to make a fight out of it, he had to stay alive.

Lifting the lamp from the bracket, he stepped into the room that had been his bedroom and for a moment stood looking at the picture of his mother that was propped up on his bureau. It had been taken less than a year before her death. In many ways he favored her, but for the first time in his life, he realized how much he favored his father, not in looks so much as in disposition. The stubborn streak that kept him from taking Bess's offer and leaving the mesa had certainly come from his father. Bess had probably threatened him, too, but John Roland had stayed. The picture was small enough that he could put it in his back pocket.

Returning to the kitchen, Clay blew out the lamp and set it back in the bracket. He went into the front room and, blowing out the lamp on the claw-footed table, left the house. When he reached the barn, he found Ardis waiting for him.

"Ready to go?" she asked.

"I'm ready," he said, and, stepping into the saddle, rode west toward the gorge, Ardis beside him.

Chapter Thirteen

Bess Flagg lay in bed, the lamp on the stand beside her turned low. She couldn't sleep and she probably wouldn't until Riley Quinn returned. Actually she didn't want to sleep. She told herself it was better to stay awake so she could feel her hate for Clay Roland.

She didn't feel anything when she was asleep. That made sleeping a waste of time. She didn't even dream any more. She was glad of that. In her last dream John Roland had been alive.

The only emotion that gave any meaning to her life was hate, but it was hard to hate a dead man, and John Roland was dead. Riley Quinn and a cowhand named Ives had taken care of that, but she wondered if it had been a mistake.

If John Roland were alive, she could have kept on punishing him. Now that he was dead, he was out of her reach. But mistake or not, she had no regrets. He had rejected her and rejection was one of several things she could not bear. He had paid for it by dying, and soon his son would pay, too.

She glanced at the clock on the wall. Almost midnight. Quinn should be back soon. She folded her hands over her breasts. They were as round and firm as ever, but she hated her helpless, atrophied legs and kept her hands away from them as much as possible.

She worried about being so helpless that she had to depend upon Ellie and Linda for the most animal-like functions of life. She was half alive and half dead, and she hated the part that was dead. She had reason for hating John Roland. He was responsible for the killing of the part of her that was dead.

She hated Linda Stevens, too, hated her for her youth and beauty and her graceful way of moving. She hated her because a man like Bill Land was willing to marry her, because Clay Roland had once loved her and maybe still did. Lately she had noticed the way Lavine was looking at Linda. He loved her, too. It was incredible and for some reason shocking, the idea that a man of Lavine's age, a man who killed for hire, could love Linda Stevens.

She closed her eyes, weary with life and the few pleasures it had given her. She could put her finger on what was wrong. She had never loved anyone, and as far as she knew she had never been loved by anyone. Oh, years ago Hank Flagg had said he loved her, but what merit was there in being loved by a tobacco-chewing old man who drank too much and shaved once a week and stunk like a wolfer?

John Roland could have given some meaning to her life. That was why she hated him so much.

There had been a time when she thought she had loved him, but now she was convinced that it had been an illusion, that she had no capacity for love. Probably she never had. She had been able to control everyone else, everyone except John Roland, and he had stayed out of her reach in spite of anything she could do.

She dropped off into a light sleep for a few minutes. When she woke, she heard Riley Quinn putting his horse away. Ives and Bellew should be with him, but she didn't hear them talking. That made her uneasy. Maybe Clay Roland had killed both of them. If he had, she had little hope that Quinn had done the job by himself.

Presently she heard Quinn's heavy steps as he came through the back of the house and crossed the kitchen to her room. A moment later he stood beside her bed, looking down at her, an ugly expression on his sun-reddened face. She knew before he opened his mouth that he had failed.

"So you let him slip between your fingers?" she said.

"How'd you know?"

"I could read it in your face," she said. "You have an easy face to read, Riley."

"Don't give me any of your smart talk," he said sullenly. "We tried. By God, we tried the best we could. He had the house all lit up and we figured he was inside. We was going in both doors so we'd have him bottled up, but he opened up on us from the barn. Bellew got hit, but he didn't quit. We was going after him when somebody else started shooting at us from the river. They had us in a crossfire, so we pulled out."

"Was it Mattson?"

"Hell, how would I know? I figured it was, though. I can't think of nobody else who would side Roland."

"How bad's Bellew hurt?"

"Got a slug in his thigh. He was bleeding some when I left him, so I sent Ives to town with him to see that he made it to the doc."

She shook her head, thinking that she had to depend on someone else's legs and in the past Riley Quinn's had served her well. But he was stupid or he wouldn't have gone at this job the way he had. He was like a bull. The only way he knew how to do anything was to lower his head and charge.

"All right," he said irritably. "Don't tell me I don't have a brain in my head. I'm the best you've got and don't you forget it."

"I won't, Riley," she said.

"I'll get him tomorrow," he said. "I'll take the crew. If I'd done it this time, we'd have had him."

"So it's my fault because I told you to take two men," she said. "Maybe so, but three men ought to be able to handle even a hardcase like Clay Roland. The fewer men who know what's going on, the better for us. You know that."

"Yea, I reckon I do," he grumbled, "but now he'll run and we'll have to chase him, and it'll be a hell of a tough job if he heads for the Smoky Hills, which same I figure he'll do."

She nodded. "He will if he's got Mattson with him."

"We'll get him if it takes a week." He turned toward the door, then thought of something and swung back. "How much longer are you gonna keep them two gunslinging bastards on your payroll?"

"I'll fire them the day Clay Roland dies," she said. "We won't need them any longer."

"We don't need 'em now," he said. "We never did."

"They've been useful," she said. "I thought we could lay Clay Roland's death on them, but we can't now."

He took a hitch on his belt, licked his lips, then blurted: "Bess, I've asked you before to marry me. I ain't gonna keep on asking you any more'n I'm gonna keep on risking my neck and working my tail off just being your hired man. You put me off once more and I'm riding out of here, and to hell with Mister Clay Roland."

"Afraid, Riley?" she asked softly.

"You know damned well I ain't."

"Marrying me would make you a rich man," she said, "but I couldn't be a real wife, so I don't see why you want me."

"Reason enough," he said.

She smiled mockingly. "I suppose that with all the money you'd have, you could find plenty of women. You'd bring one right out here under my nose probably. But maybe you wouldn't have to. Linda would do, wouldn't she?"

"By God, Bess," he said in a tone of utter frustration, "I ought to twist your neck. You can be a real bitch when you set your mind to it. I've talked to Doc Spears about you. He said there's nothing wrong with you that would keep you from being all the wife a man would want. I'd never bring a woman here, and, if I did, I wouldn't settle for a skinny one like Linda."

She masked her face against the worry that his words had aroused in her. Riley Quinn and Ellie were two people she could not do without. In a way she liked Riley. Usually he succeeded in his bumbling way in doing what she asked him to do, and he seldom questioned her decisions. Being married to him wouldn't be so bad. She could handle him.

"I'm glad to hear that, Riley," she said. "Linda wouldn't be a good woman for you. I don't think she's good for any man."

"You hate her like you hate everybody else," he said bitterly. "What's the matter with you, Bess? Sometimes I think you live on hate. It's what keeps you alive."

"I suppose it is," she admitted, "but I don't hate

137

you, Riley. I guess we belong together. We're a lot alike. At least we're not hypocrites. I'm glad you didn't give me any of the hogwash about loving me the way most men would. I know you don't and you know I don't love you, so we can start out being honest with each other. If you understand that, I'll marry you."

"When?"

"The day Clay Roland dies."

He shook his head in disgust. "I knew you'd get around to something like that. You're no good, Bess. Neither am I."

"That's funny, Riley," she murmured. "I didn't think you had any more notion about being good than I do."

He cursed and, wheeling, ponderously walked to the door, his spurs jingling. He turned back, scowling. "You better send for the preacher 'cause it won't take me long to cut Roland's ears off and fetch 'em back to you."

He left the room. A moment later she heard the back door slam shut. She lay on her back, her hands still folded over her breasts, smiling a little as if she enjoyed a private joke. Doc Spears was right. *She* could be a wife to a man, and she would if it meant keeping Riley Quinn.

She could keep Riley in line, she told herself. By using him and Bill Land, she could handle anyone else on the mesa. This was the one pleasure of a life that had become a burden, controlling able-bodied men who didn't need to use someone else's legs, controlling them and breaking them and, yes, even killing them.

She dropped off to sleep, the small smile still on her lips.

Chapter Fourteen

The overcast had cleared away and a moon was showing above the rim to the east when Clay and Ardis rode out of the gorge into her yard, the dark bulk of the buildings looming ahead of them. No lights showed in the house, so apparently Monroe had not returned with Rusty Mattson.

Ardis found a lantern in the barn and lit it. She stayed with Clay while he took care of the horses, and then, lifting the lantern off the peg where she had hung it, she walked beside him to the house.

"If you're hungry, I'll fix something to eat before we go to bed," she said.

"No, I'm not hungry."

"Want a drink?"

"No thanks. I'm ready to roll in."

They went into the dining room. Ardis lit a lamp and handed it to Clay. "The same room you had." She hesitated, her eyes searching his face, then said: "How much time do you think we have?"

"Not more'n a few hours after daylight," he said, "if I'm figuring Quinn right."

"They'll go to the Bar C, then come here," she said. "Is that the way you're guessing?"

"That's it. Riley Quinn isn't very smart, but Bess is."

"Then we'll have an early breakfast and ride out whether Rusty's here or not," she said.

He nodded. "Looks like we'd better." He thought of urging her to stay here, but he didn't think she would. Besides, this would be a more dangerous place for her to stay than on the trail with him. He still thought of her as a tomboy, saucy and impetuous as she had been six years ago, but now, his gaze on her face, it struck him that she wasn't the same girl he remembered. This startled him. Linda hadn't really changed, but Ardis had. Her piquant face was shadowed by worry. Fear, too, perhaps.

Impulsively he put out both hands and gripped her shoulders. "Ardis, why don't you give up this business of punishing your father's killers?"

She swayed toward him, her lips parted, then checked herself. "Will you give up the Bar C?"

"No. I can't."

"Then you know the answer to your question." She turned away, calling back: "Good night, Clay!"

He went upstairs, placed the lamp on the pine bureau, and sat down on the bed. He tugged off his boots, then laid his gun belt on a chair beside the head of the bed. He blew the lamp out and lay down, tired and sour-tempered. Tomorrow he would start running and ducking and hiding. Nothing went against his grain as much as that.

He had to find a place where Ardis would be

safe. He might have to cross the Utah line to find such a place. He certainly couldn't keep her with him indefinitely. She would slow him down, and if the Flagg bunch cornered him and there was a finish fight, he couldn't expose her to danger.

She was obsessed by revenge, he thought, and that again wasn't like the girl he remembered. When he used to come here, he had talked with her very little. Rusty was the one she had been interested in, with a good deal of joshing going on back and forth between them, while Clay laughed and Long Sam Kline listened with concern because he didn't want Rusty for a son-in-law.

Now it was different, with Long Sam dead. If she was in love with Rusty, they should be married. Rusty had certainly been fond enough of her. It was one reason he used to come here. He dropped off to sleep, still wondering what kept them apart.

Clay was aroused by the tap of Ardis's knuckles on the door. She called: "Breakfast will be ready in a little while! I thought you'd want to feed the horses before we eat."

"I just got to sleep," he complained.

"It's after five," she said.

"All right." He sat up and yawned. "I'll get dressed."

When he returned from the barn a few minutes

later, she had two bowls of oatmeal mush and a platter of ham and eggs on the kitchen table. She poured the coffee as Clay sat down. This morning she was wearing a man's shirt and pants; her auburn hair was brushed back and pinned in a bun behind her head. The worry that had been so noticeable in her last night was gone. She looked fresh and slim and young, and it struck him that she was an uncommonly pretty girl.

"You look mighty pert not to have slept much last night," he said. "How do you do it?"

She laughed. "Just being with you, I guess."

"I thought you and Rusty would be married before now," he said.

She looked up from her plate, startled. "Not Rusty. He'd never be tied down by a woman. He's the most restless man I ever knew. He's on the go all the time. Nothing seems important to him."

They ate in silence after that, Clay thinking that Rusty must have lost his common sense in the last six years. A man would have to be crazy to become a drifter when he could settle down with Ardis Kline.

They were finishing when someone shouted from in front of the house. "They're here," Ardis said, and jumped up.

Clay followed her outside. Monroe was watering the horses and Rusty was walking toward the house. When he saw Clay, he let out a war whoop. "You old horse thief!" he yelled, and strode toward Clay, his hand extended. "Damned if it ain't been a long time." He shook Clay's hand and pounded him on the back. "Yes, sir, a long time. You've made yourself a big man from what I hear."

Clay shook his head. "Not on this range."

"Then we'll change it." Rusty whacked him on the back again. "You look just like you used to, son. I sure have been wondering about that. You've been away and you seen the elephant, and now you're back, but you still look just the same. Hell, I thought maybe you'd've growed a set of horns and a tail by now."

"They're there," Clay said. "You just don't see them, Rusty. You're the same, too. Maybe a little thinner. That's all."

He was lying and he was sure Rusty knew he was. He couldn't tell Rusty how much he had changed. Clay was stunned by it. Rusty had the look of the wild bunch on him. Clay had seen it in too many men to be mistaken. It was typical of the men who lived in the Smoky Hills, but still it shocked Clay to see it so plainly in Rusty.

Actually this was not a thing Clay could describe except in the way Rusty's thin lips set hard against his teeth. The furtive darting about of his eyes, too. But mostly it was a feeling Clay had of wildness in the man as if he cared nothing about anyone or anything.

There was this moment of uneasy silence, then Ardis said: "I'll cook breakfast for you, Rusty. Clay thinks we'd better get started."

"I'm hungry enough to eat," Rusty said. "A whole cow if you've got one."

"I'll call you when it's ready," she said, and ran into the house.

For a moment Clay and Rusty looked at each other, Rusty's thin, stubble-covered face grave. Finally he said: "All right, son. Tell me what you see."

"A man on the run," Clay said. "I'll look the same in a few days. I'm on the run, too. But what are you running from?"

"From myself," Rusty said. "From all the things I might have been and the things we used to dream about being. You went out and done 'em, but me, I just went to pot." He grinned and shrugged his skinny shoulders. "Well, it's a little more'n that. I'm running from Queen Bess same as you are. Maybe you heard she posted me off the mesa."

"I heard," Clay said, "but there's other places in the world than the mesa and Painted Rock and the Smoky Hills."

"I've been to a few of 'em, but none of 'em would do," Rusty said. "You seen the great man since you got back?"

"Who's that?"

"Honest Bill Land, the legal voice of Bess Flagg."

"I've seen him." Clay hesitated, then told him what had happened in town.

Rusty slapped his leg and guffawed. "I wish I could've watched that. He's had a licking coming for a long time. He's sold out, Clay. Sold his soul to that bitch of a Bess Flagg."

"Is he in love with Linda?"

"Love?" Rusty snorted in derision. "Son, he don't know the meaning of the word. Neither does Linda. She wants a husband who's important like a lawyer, and Bill, bless his shriveled little heart, wants to sleep warm in the winter, and if his woman's got Bess Flagg's blessing, that's all the better."

Ardis called from the porch: "It's ready, Rusty!"

They went into the dining room. Rusty tossed his dusty hat on a table and followed Ardis into the kitchen. He sat down and wolfed his food as if he hadn't eaten for twenty-four hours. Perhaps he hadn't, Clay thought. From his appearance Clay judged Rusty hadn't eaten well for a long time.

"I'm in trouble," Clay said. "I guess you know about Dad's death and Bess's saying she's taken over the Bar C."

"Sure, we've all heard it."

"Well, it wasn't my idea to send for you. I mean, if you side me, you'll be in trouble, too."

"You're trying to say you don't want me?"

"No, I'm not saying that at all. I'd be proud to

146

have your help, but I'll have Riley Quinn on my tail. Before long, I think. Ardis says she's going with me, so I've got to get her to some place that'll be safe."

"She'll stick with you." Rusty looked around. "Where'd she go?"

"Outside to tell Monroe to saddle up for us, I guess. She helped me out of a hole last night when Quinn came after me." He told what happened at the Bar C, then added: "Damn it, Rusty, I don't want either one of you killed or hurt on account of me."

Rusty sat back, chewing on a mouthful of ham. He swallowed it, then said: "We're in trouble already, Clay, Ardis and me both. It's always been a question of time until they burn this place and hunt down every one of us who live in the hills. We do some rustling. Enough to keep us eating. That's about all. So what happens? They treat us like dirt. Posting me off the mesa, for instance. They don't want us coming into Painted Rock. Not any of us."

He waggled a finger at Clay. "It's more'n your hide or mine, son. There's plenty of people on the mesa who would like to see Bess cut down to size. They've needed somebody like you for a long time."

"Well, then," Clay said, "I guess the main thing is to stay alive."

"That's right," Rusty agreed. "Monroe will stay

here. I don't like it much, but that's what he says he's gonna do. But Ardis now, you've got to keep them sons-of-bitches from getting their hands on her. They ain't forgot she's Long Sam's girl and they figure she's doing all that they used to accuse him of doing."

"Is she?"

"Hell no. Sam never done 'em, neither."

Rusty gave him an angry glance and Clay wished he hadn't asked the question. Ardis came in a moment later and, going into the pantry, filled a flour sack with food. When she came to the table, she said: "The horses are ready."

Rusty picked up the last piece of ham from the platter and shoved it into his mouth as he rose. "We're ready."

Ardis took a Mackinaw off the wall by the back door, put on her hat, and left the house. Rusty glanced at Clay. He said softly: "She's real, son. She ain't like Linda who used to lead you around by the nose."

Clay followed Rusty outside. A moment later they mounted. Ardis lingered to say something to Monroe, then they started climbing the ridge to the west, the buildings soon lost to sight as the cedars and piñons closed in around them.

Chapter Fifteen

Bess Flagg slept fitfully until dawn, awaking in time to hear the crew going to breakfast. She stared at the ceiling as the first gray light crept through the window and slowly became brighter until she could see across the room. This was the hour when she usually called Ellie in from the kitchen and Ellie would help her dress and lift her into the wheelchair and push her to the table for breakfast, but today it was different. She wanted to watch the crew leave and she couldn't see the yard from the kitchen.

She turned her head toward the window in time to see Lavine and Reno leave the bunkhouse and go to breakfast. A moment later Riley Quinn and the crew left the cook shack and drifted across the yard to the corral where they gathered to listen to Quinn. She could see what was happening, for now the sun had tipped up above the peaks of the San Juans and was laying its first sharp rays upon the dust of the yard.

Bess wished she could hear what was being said. She could see there was an argument and she could guess what it was about. Every cowboy out there resented Lavine's and Reno's presence. Quinn had told her that more than once. The way they saw it, Lavine and Reno didn't work, but they drew fighting wages while the cowhands received the regular $40 a month and found. Now they were probably saying that if there was fighting to be done, let Lavine and Reno do it.

They had a sound argument, Bess admitted to herself. She wished that she had never hired Lavine and Reno, but that was water over the dam. She'd let them go in a day or two. Right now Quinn would have to make his orders stick or he was finished. He knew that. He had absolutely no finesse, but he had brute strength. So far that had been enough.

By the time Lavine and Reno left the cook shack, the crew had saddled up. Quinn said something to Lavine, and Lavine said something back, then Reno got into the argument. Lavine wheeled and slapped him across the face, spinning the younger man half around. Reno backed off, right hand poised above his gun. Lavine watched contemptuously until he turned and went into the bunkhouse, his head down.

Quinn and his men mounted and struck off in a southwesterly direction, some of the horses bucking until they were pulled down by the steady hands of their riders. She didn't have a poor cowboy in the crew. She could thank Quinn for that. The poor ones didn't last.

At times she wondered why any of the men stayed, with Quinn working them as hard as he did. It wasn't the wages she paid. Maybe it was pride in working for the Flagg outfit. They had a status on the mesa that lifted them above the cowhands who worked for the run-of-the-mill neighboring ranches. Bess liked to think that was important to them.

She reached for the bell that was on her night stand and rang it. A moment later Ellie came in with a towel, a washcloth, and a basin of hot water. " 'Mornin', Miz Flagg," Ellie said. "You slept later'n usual."

"I haven't been asleep," Bess said. "Linda up?"

"No, ma'am."

Ellie helped Bess sit up and braced her back with pillows, then placed the basin of water on her lap. Bess said: "Get Linda up. There's no room on this ranch for sleepy-heads."

"Yes, ma'am," Ellie said. "I'll get her up right away."

Bess washed, set the basin on the bed beside her, and, taking her brush and comb from the night stand, began brushing her hair. She hated Linda so much that it was hard at times to be pleasant, but she always had maintained the fiction of being fond of Linda, or nearly always, often enough that Linda was not likely to leave.

Now it was time to force the situation with Bill Land. She laughed as she thought about it. Neither Linda nor Bill wanted to get married, but they would because she told them to. They'd have a hell of a married life, she told herself, once they started living together.

Bess laughed again, thinking how much she would enjoy having the wedding in her parlor. Everyone was a puppet in her hands if she could find the string, and she always could if she had time. John Roland was the one exception. She swore and slammed the brush down on the night stand. John was the one great failure even though she had tried harder with him than she had ever tried with anyone else.

Ellie came in, saying: "Linda's dressin'. She'll be down in a minute."

"Help me dress," Bess ordered, "and then get me into that damned chair. The morning's half gone."

"Yes, ma'am," Ellie said.

Bess was almost finished with her breakfast when Linda came down the stairs from her room. She said: "I'm sorry, Bess. I guess I over-slept."

"I guess you did." Bess leaned back in the wheelchair, her coffee cup in her hand. "Linda, you've been shilly-shallying around with Bill long enough. I've got my heart set on having your wedding right here in this house. Don't put it off any longer. I'll send for Bill and we'll set the date." She smiled. "Maybe for this afternoon."

Linda sat down at the table and dipped her spoon into the sugar. Without looking up, she said: "All right, Bess. You go ahead and send for him."

"Good," Bess said, and motioned for Ellie to fill her cup.

Bess drank her coffee slowly, assuming an expression of bland interest as she watched Linda eat her breakfast, but all the time her mind was working in another direction. She would have to get along without Riley Quinn for two or three days and she didn't trust Abe Lavine. Pete Reno was just a punk kid who had no brains, so she couldn't depend on him. She should have got rid of them a long time ago, and she would have if she hadn't thought she'd need them to cut down Clay Roland.

As it turned out, Lavine was too cute with his planning and talking about the right time to do a job like that. Maybe he was afraid of Roland. In any case she had been forced to send Quinn after Roland, but she didn't want to be left without a man on the ranch, so she'd keep Lavine and Reno until Quinn got back. That left no one she could trust but Slim Ives, and he'd probably be back early this morning.

"Wheel me out to the front porch," she said to Ellie. "Fetch my sweater and my binoculars. You go ahead and finish breakfast, Linda. I've got some thinking to do and I can do it better if I'm alone."

She thought Linda looked relieved. She

wondered why, and then put it out of her mind. When Ellie rolled her out through the front door to the porch, she found the morning air chillier than she had expected and told Ellie to bring a blanket. She raised the binoculars to her eyes and studied the road to town. A rider was coming in and a moment later she saw it was Slim Ives.

Ellie returned with a blanket and tucked it around Bess's shoulders. "Go back and clean up the kitchen," Bess said. "I'll be all right now."

"Yes, ma'am," Ellie said, and retreated to the back of the house.

Bess waited with impatience until Ives came within hailing distance. At times like this when she was eager to do something, her helplessness made her physically sick. For years she had prided herself on being as capable as any man, going where she wanted and doing what she wanted without asking for help from anyone. Now she was dependent upon an ordinary cowhand just to go to town.

When she called to him, Ives reined over to the porch and touched the brim of his hat to her. He said: " 'Mornin', Missus Flagg. Riley gone yet?"

"He took the crew and went after Roland," she said. "How's Bellew?"

"Weak," Ives said. "He lost a lot of blood before I got him to town, but Doc Spears says he'll make it. Well, I guess I better see if I can catch up with Riley."

"No hurry about that," she said. "I want you to harness up the wagon and take me to town."

He hesitated, letting his face show his distaste for the job, then he said reluctantly—"Yes, ma'am."—and rode on to the corral.

A few minutes later he was back with the wagon. Bess called Ellie from the house, and Ellie rolled the chair down the ramp that had been built for her alongside the steps.

"Lift me up to the seat," she ordered Ives, "then tie the chair down in the wagon bed so it won't roll."

He obeyed, and when he stepped into the seat beside her, she was holding the lines. "I'll drive," she said. "Been quite a while since I drove a team. Ellie, you tell Linda I won't be back for a spell. I have some errands to run."

"Yes, ma'am, I'll tell her," Ellie said, and, turning, trudged into the house.

Ives was normally a silent man and now he seemed embarrassed by having to sit beside Bess. She looked at him, amused. He was tall and slim, with a knobby, scarred face that gave him a tough look. She was a good judge of men, and she had a feeling he was just as tough as he appeared to be. She knew Quinn trusted him completely, that he had been taken along every time she had given Quinn a dirty job to do.

Ives received the same wages the rest of the men did. He must have something in mind or he wouldn't stay. Maybe Quinn had told him that sooner or later he'd marry the boss and Ives would be foreman. Well, it didn't make any difference. She would use him as long as she could. She'd use Quinn, too. She could play hard to get with him as well as Linda could play it with Bill Land.

When they reached town, Bess stopped in front of the drugstore and told Ives to ask Land to come down. When the lawyer appeared a moment later, she was shocked by the bruised and battered condition of his face.

"Good morning, Bess," Land said, and stood waiting for her to tell him what she wanted.

"My God, Bill," she whispered. "Did Roland do that to you?"

"He sure as hell did," Land said. "If I ever see him again, I'll kill him."

"That's a chore you won't have to do," she said. "Riley has taken the crew and gone after him. He tried last night and missed. Bellew got shot in the fracas."

"So I heard," Land said.

Bess glanced at Ives who discreetly remained at the foot of the stairs. She said: "Tell me exactly what happened between you and Roland."

Land obeyed, not sparing himself, then he said: "Clay was always better'n me with his hands. I

156

should have plugged him." He paused, running the tip of his tongue over his swollen lips, then he said: "I won't marry Linda, Bess. She's a bitch. You should have seen the way she kissed him. She's been in love with him all this time. And then that damned Lavine comes running up, saying he'll kill me if I plug Clay."

Bess nodded, a slow fury beginning to burn in her as she compared Land's story with what Lavine and Linda had told her when they had got back from town. Well, she'd attend to them later when she got home.

"I don't like to be made a fool of any more than you do, Bill," she said, "but you're marrying Linda and you're going to tame her. Chances are she's had her mind on Clay Roland all these years, but she'll forget him when he's dead and she's your wife."

Land said nothing. He stood, staring at his feet. Sensing his silent resistance, she said sharply: "Don't back down on me, Bill. I'll double the monthly retaining fee I pay you and I'll get you into the legislature, but you've got to get one thing through your head. If you want my help, you'll do what I tell you."

"But why have I got to marry Linda?" he demanded.

"Because I'm fond of her," Bess said blandly, "and because I want you to have a woman who is attractive and will help advance your career.

I've got big plans for you, Bill, and they include Linda."

"All right," he muttered, his gaze still on the ground.

"Fine," she said brightly. "I think we'd better get this knot tied *pronto*. Get the preacher and fetch him out right after dinner."

"The preacher's out of town," Land said uneasily. "He won't be back until evening."

"All right, bring him out first thing in the morning," she said brusquely, then called: "Ives, I'm ready to go!"

The cowboy stepped into the seat. Turning the team, she drove west down the river, not taking the turn north to her ranch. Ives asked: "Where are we going?"

"To the Bar C," she said. "It's mine. I want to look at it." He scowled, and she added quickly: "Roland won't be there. If Riley found him, he's dead long before now, but it's my guess he's lit out for the hills."

"I ain't afraid of him, Missus Flagg," Ives said sharply, "if that's what you're thinking. No use cussing Riley, but he didn't play it smart last night or we'd have nailed Roland then."

"I agree with you," she said. "Riley is a good man in a lot of ways, but like you say, he isn't always smart. I've wondered about John Roland and Sam Kline. Was it yours or Riley's idea to take care of them the way you did?"

"Mine," he said. "Maybe you don't know it, but rubbing Kline out was a mistake. He wasn't doing us no hurt."

"His place was a hang-out for thieves and rustlers," she said sharply. "I'm glad he's gone." She gave Ives a long, speculative glance, then she said: "I might have known you were the one who figured how to handle them. I guess I've been overlooking a good man, so I'll see that the situation is remedied."

"It's about time," he said, glancing at her as if not sure how to take what she had said.

"Yes, it is," she agreed amiably. "I've left too many things in Riley's hands."

"Lavine's and Reno's, too," he said angrily.

"I'm getting rid of them in a day or two," she said. "Just as soon as Riley gets back."

He was silent until they reached the Bar C. She pulled the team to a stop, her gaze sweeping this place where she had come so often when she had been pursuing John Roland. Bitterness clouded her mind as she thought about the foolish things she had done, the only time in her life when she had been foolish that way.

She had loved him, all right. That was the only reason she would ever have done what she had. The truth was she had never been completely honest with herself before. Now she was here again to torture herself with painful memories, but it was the last time.

"Take the chair down and put me in it," she said. "I want to go inside."

He hesitated, not understanding what was in her mind, but he obeyed. He wheeled her into the house. For a moment she sat looking around. Nothing was changed. The room was as familiar as her own parlor. Even the chessmen and the board on the claw-footed table in the middle of the room had been there the last time she was here.

She considered how it might have been between her and John Roland, how she thought it was going to be for a long time. Then she remembered their quarrel. She had not been able to stand being put off any longer and she had asked him to marry her. He had gone into a bedroom and come out with his wife's picture.

"I married her forever," John Roland had said. "I'll never marry you or anyone else."

He had never said that to her before. She had been so sure she could wear him down sooner or later, but she had failed. There had been a furious argument, and finally she'd lost her temper and slapped him, then he'd pushed her out through the front door and locked it.

The frustrating memory of her broken dreams crowded into her mind, hurting her with an agony she had never thought she would feel again. "Damn him!" she cried out. "God damn him!" Her hand came out in a violent gesture and swept the chessmen off the board and sent them banging against the wall. She grabbed up the board and ripped it down the middle, and slammed the pieces down. She snatched up the lamp and threw it against the floor, the glass breaking. She watched the coal oil flow across the boards; she caught the smell of it and she began to cry.

"Light it!" she screamed, and swiped a sleeve across her eyes. "Damn it, burn the house down!"

He obeyed, still puzzled by her behavior. For a moment she watched the flames creep along the floor. She thought about loving John Roland and then killing him. Now she would burn all that was left of him. Riley Quinn would destroy his son. Then she thought of Linda. Maybe the girl still loved Clay Roland. She must, from what Bill Land had said. Then Bess would destroy her, too, just as she was destroying this house.

"Wheel me outside and put me in the wagon," she said. "You drive."

She did not look back at the burning house as the wagon climbed out of the valley. All of this was behind her. It was gone, wiped out. That was the way it would stay. In the end she would destroy John Roland, root and branch. Even the memory of him would be gone. It would be as if he had never lived.

Chapter Sixteen

Near midmorning Clay, Ardis, and Mattson reached a high point on the ridge west of Storm River. They pulled up to let their horses blow and dismounted, Mattson stretching and yawning as he looked down at the buildings of the Kline place, reduced to toy size by the distance.

"I've got a hunch we didn't get away none too soon," Mattson said. "By dark we'll have Flagg riders all through these hills."

"Sooner than that," Ardis said, and, walking up the trail, disappeared into a thicket of cedars.

Clay's gaze followed her until she was out of sight, thinking that in the men's clothes and heavy Mackinaw she was wearing, she was still completely feminine. He said: "Funny thing, Rusty. Before I left, I thought she was just a harebrained kid, more boy than girl. When I first got back, I kept seeing her the same way, but I was wrong. She's a woman."

"A hell of a lot of woman," Mattson said. "What are you fixing to do with her?"

"I don't know," Clay said. "The only reason I let her come was because I figured she wouldn't be safe at home when Quinn got there. I was hoping I could talk her into going on into Utah and staying till this is over."

"She won't do it," Mattson said. "She's as good as any man when it comes to riding through these hills, and she can shoot as straight, too. She figures you need her, so she'll stick with you."

Clay nodded, thinking that Rusty was right. He said: "I remember how you used to josh her and she'd come right back at you. I thought you two would be married before now."

Rusty had started to roll a cigarette. Now he stopped, the paper curling in his fingers as he stared at Clay. "My God, man, have you gone daft? It's always been you from the time we first started coming to her place. She's had a dozen men after her to marry them, some pretty good men that Long Sam liked and figured would make good husbands for her. She never told her pa how she felt about you, but she's told me plenty of times. Whenever I showed up, she always asked if I'd heard from you or heard anything about you. Then she'd ask me if I figured you'd be coming back someday, but hell, I couldn't answer her. How would I know what a man like you was going to do?"

Clay turned away. His first thought was that Rusty was mistaken, but he knew almost immediately that his friend was right. If he hadn't been blind, he would have known. A woman wouldn't be doing what Ardis was if she didn't love him. He would have known before this, if Linda hadn't filled his thoughts the way she had.

Rusty sealed the cigarette and lit it. He said: "I reckon this ain't anything you want to hear, but you're going to hear it. Linda wouldn't have been good for you. She was flirting on the side with every man she could. The only reason she had any time for you was because she figured you could take her to the Bar C and support her. After your pa kicked you out, she was done with you."

Clay whirled on Rusty, wanting to tell him he was wrong. A woman couldn't kiss a man the way Linda had kissed him in town if she didn't love him. But loving him and marrying him were two different things. Rusty was right. Linda had probably never had a serious thought about anyone except herself. Well, it didn't make any difference. He had put her out of his life forever.

Ardis was coming toward them down the trail, walking rapidly and gracefully. Clay, watching her, was struck by a great wave of feeling for her. She had asked nothing of him, but she was willing to give anything. Rusty was right. He had been blind.

When she joined them, Rusty was staring at the river far below them. He asked: "Where are you taking Clay?"

"To the stone cabin," she said. "It's the safest place I know. I thought about trying to get a bunch of the hills men together to fight Quinn, but it's not their fight."

"I figured we'd keep going across the line and

find a place where you'd be safe," Clay said. "Moab, maybe."

She shook her head defiantly, her lips tightly pressed against her teeth. "I don't want to be safe. If you're going to Utah, I'll go with you. If you come back, I'll be with you. I won't let you fight the whole Flagg crew by yourself."

One look at her face told him there was no use to argue with her. They'd probably be safe enough in the stone cabin, wherever that was. He said: "All right, we'll go to the stone cabin."

"We'd better ride," she said, irritated by his suggestion that they go on into Utah.

"Take a look down there," Mattson said. "They ain't far behind us."

Clay saw the riders pouring out of the gorge. They were too far away to be recognized, but Clay did not doubt that it was the Flagg crew, Riley Quinn riding in front.

"They've made good time," Clay said.

"They sure have," Rusty agreed. "That's Quinn for you. He's been pushing those boys since breakfast and no mistake."

"How far is it to the stone cabin?" Clay asked.

"We'll be there by noon," Ardis said, "or a little after."

"You tell Monroe where you're headed?" Mattson asked.

She nodded. "He won't tell them."

"No, reckon he won't," Rusty conceded, "but

chances are they'll beat hell out of him trying to make him tell. Don't make no difference if he does. Quinn will have that half-breed, Pete Blackdog, with him, and Pete can track a fly across the top of a table."

Ardis pinned her gaze on Clay's face. "I expect them to find us. We can keep running and I think we could stay ahead of them, but it seems to me it's better to let them find us. If we hole up in the stone cabin, we can cut them up. I don't think it will take much of a loss to pull them off."

"How do you figure that?" Clay asked.

"What makes men fight?" she countered. "I mean, want to fight enough to die?"

"A lot of reasons," Clay answered. "Duty. Loyalty. Money, maybe. All depends on the man."

"Sure it does," she said, "but do the men who are following Riley Quinn have a sense of duty that makes them want to fight you? Are they loyal to Queen Bess or to Quinn? Are they getting big pay to run you down and risk their lives?"

"I don't know about the pay . . . ," Clay began.

"I do," Rusty said. "Bess pays Lavine and Reno fighting wages, but not the crew. What she don't know is that she hurt herself with every man on her crew when she hired them gunslicks."

"You know more about these things than I do, Clay," Ardis said, "so you can tell me if I'm wrong, but it seems to me that if we could knock

166

a couple of them out of their saddles, and we were holed up in the stone cabin where they couldn't get at us, they wouldn't have much stomach for fighting."

"You never know for sure how men are going to perform in a fight," Clay said, "but the chances are you're right."

"We're wasting time," Rusty said impatiently. "Won't take 'em long to find us once they start up the ridge."

They mounted and rode west, the trail dipping and turning around tall upthrusts of red rock. At times they crossed open areas fifty acres or more in size, the grass brown and dry. Twice they spooked big bucks that went bounding off into the cedars, and occasionally they rode past small bands of cattle. Some of the brands had unquestionably been worked over, but if Rusty noticed, he said nothing. Clay wondered if the Bar C herd was somewhere here in the Smoky Hills.

They reached a fork in the trail and reined up. This was where Clay had taken the wrong trail on his way in and had wound up down on the river below the Kline place. If he had turned right instead of left, he would have stayed on top of the ridge as they had just done and so saved himself at least an hour of time and several miles of riding.

"The stone cabin's three, four miles ahead and

off to the south," Rusty said. "We ain't gonna hide our tracks less'n we put wings on these horses. Now the way I figure, it's gonna be tough fighting the whole outfit, but if you were bucking just half of 'em, you could discourage 'em like Ardis said."

"If you're driving at what I think you are," Clay said, "I'm against it."

"So am I," Ardis said. "If we separate, we'll make the same mistake Custer did. Ever hear what happened to him, Rusty?"

"Seems like I did." Rusty grinned and winked at her. "But this is different. I wouldn't think of busting up if we was on the mesa, but I'm supposed to be safe around here. Now they're gonna be some puzzled when our tracks split. Monroe will tell 'em Ardis is with us. They may think she went that way"—he nodded at the left fork—"figuring she'll circle back home. But Quinn won't be sure. He might just as easy think it's you, Clay, wanting to duck around 'em and double back to the mesa. But whatever they think, they're gonna divide up. Sooner or later they'll get together, but meantime you won't be fighting more'n half the crew. I reckon you can handle that many if you're the man I think you are, Clay."

"Sure," Clay said, "but what about you?"

"They won't hurt me if they do find me," Rusty said. "Not when they're chasing you. I'll ride

168

down the trail a piece, then take off through the cedars. I'll make camp somewhere down yonder and go to sleep. I'm about all in."

Clay still didn't like it. He doubted that Rusty was as all in as he claimed. Six years ago Rusty could have ridden two days and one night without being worn out and Clay didn't think the years had changed him that much.

"I'm still against it," Clay said. "I say to stick together."

Ardis scratched the back of her neck, frowning as her gaze turned from one man to the other. Finally she said: "Clay's right. Sometimes Quinn goes as crazy mad as Queen Bess does. You know that as well as I do."

"I'm going this way." Rusty jerked his hand to the north. "You can do what you want to, but I ain't sitting here all day arguing about it."

"I guess we can't stop you," Ardis said. "Looks like you want out of it."

"Sure I do." Rusty grinned at her again. "You two can do the fighting. Me, I don't cotton to the notion of stopping any Flagg lead."

He whirled his horse around and rode off, following the north fork of the trail. He looked back once to wave, then disappeared down the slope among the cedars.

"He's lying," Clay said. "He wants to get Quinn off our tail, and he's going to get himself killed doing it."

"I'm sorry I said what I did, but I've known Rusty most of my life and I get mad at him every time he has one of his stubborn spells." Ardis paused, biting her lip, then said: "We'd better mosey along."

They went on, Clay knowing exactly what Ardis had meant. Rusty had always been bull-headed on things like this. Clay remembered he used to be able to talk Bill Land out of almost anything, but he'd never changed Rusty's mind once he had decided on something he considered important.

Half an hour later they turned off the ridge and followed a narrow trail to the south that showed little recent use. It led to the bottom of a cañon that held a small, clear stream running over a red-rock bottom. They turned up the cañon, the walls steep and so close together in places that they cut off the noon-high sun. Another mile brought them into a grass-covered bowl. At the upper side to the west was the stone cabin, built on a ledge ten feet above the floor of the valley.

They rode across the bowl and dismounted below the cabin. Ardis untied the sacks of food while Clay pulled their rifles from the scabbards, then she motioned upstream. "There's a corral above the narrows," she said. "Take care of the horses while I get dinner."

"Any way out of here?" he asked. "Except the way we came in."

She smiled. "Up. That's all."

Picking up the sacks of food and the rifles, she climbed the rough steps that had been chipped out of the sandstone. Clay pulled gear from her horse, then mounted his bay and led the other animal upstream. There was nothing to do but wait, he thought, wait for Riley Quinn and the Flagg crew.

Chapter Seventeen

Riley Quinn set a hard pace from the time he left the Flagg Ranch, the crew strung out behind him. He was not a perceptive man on matters that had to do with human relationships, but even anyone as insensitive as he was could not help feeling that something was wrong between him and the crew. They had been close to rebellion back there at the corral, mostly because they had been hired to work. They said Lavine and Reno were paid to fight, so let them go after Roland and do the fighting.

Well, he'd curried them down, all right. He'd told them Queen Bess had given them the job of running Roland down, so it was up to them to show her they could do any job she gave them.

The rebellion hadn't amounted to anything, he told himself. There wasn't a man in the crew who could stand up to him in a fistfight. He'd demonstrated that on more than one occasion. The men who didn't like his methods left, the others knuckled under. Still, he was plagued by the feeling that something was different this morning. The men had turned sullen when he'd told them what they were going to do, and they remained sullen. He didn't hear a word back along the line all the way to the Bar C.

They'd get over it, he told himself. The thing to do was to keep them busy. They knew who gave the orders. Ease up on a bunch of men and some loud-mouth starts to talk, then you've got trouble. His job was to see it never got to that place.

They made a quick check of the Bar C, found it deserted, and went on down the gorge to the Kline roadhouse, Quinn confident they would find Roland there. They moved in fast and searched the buildings, but turned up no one except Monroe.

Quinn motioned to Pete Blackdog. "See if you can pick up any fresh tracks. Roland might have gone down the river, or he might have taken the trail up the ridge if he aims to get out of the state. It's my guess he ain't got more'n two, three hours start on us, so you oughtta be able to cut sign all right."

Blackdog nodded and, mounting, rode downstream. Quinn turned to Monroe. He had never seen the man before. He hadn't heard what Ardis Kline had done after her father was killed, so when Monroe said he was the girl's hired man, it was reasonable to think he was telling the truth.

"All right, Monroe, if that's your name," Quinn said, "you're going to talk. I ain't real sure Monroe is your name. You're all rustlers and horse thieves down here, and the chances are you've been riding the Owlhoot ever since you were big enough to fork a horse. It's my guess you've got to look at your hatband to see what handle you're using now."

Monroe stood in front of Quinn, a stolid, dark-faced man who was a full six inches taller than Quinn and therefore looked down at him. Quinn was always conscious of his lack of height, and to have Monroe tip his head so that he gave the appearance of looking down his nose made Quinn furious.

"It's my name," Monroe said.

"All right, all right," Quinn said harshly. "Where did Roland go when he left here?"

"I don't know," Monroe said.

Quinn hit him on the side of the head with an open palm, the sound of the blow a meaty thud like that of a butcher's cleaver on a side of beef. Monroe was spun half around, and when he turned back to look at Quinn, the side of his face that had been struck was a dull red.

"That's just a beginning," Quinn said. "I can slap you silly, and when I get tired, there's ten other men here who can work on you. If that don't do the job, we'll take your boots off and we'll fry your feet. If you stay stubborn, I'll take a knife to you. I'm the gent who taught the Apaches all they know and I ain't forgot any of it. Now talk up 'cause we're in a hell of a hurry."

"I'll tell you anything I know," Monroe said, "but all your beating and burning and knifing can't get something out of me I don't know, and I don't know where Roland went."

"Then let's hear what you do know. Roland was here last night?"

"Yeah, he was here," Monroe said. "He rode in late with Ardis. I don't know where they'd been or what they'd been doing, but Roland was here this morning. I just work for Ardis. She don't tell me all she knows or all she does."

So it had been the Kline girl who had opened up on him and Ives and Bellew from the river last night, Quinn thought, and all the time he had been so sure it was Rusty Mattson. He cursed, then caught himself. He'd be the laughingstock of the mesa if it got out that three of them had been run off the Bar C by Roland and a girl.

"Did the Kline girl go with him when he left this morning?" Quinn asked.

Monroe nodded. "Rusty Mattson was with 'em, too. He showed up this morning, ate breakfast, then lit out with the other two. Ardis, she said for me to look after things till she got back. She didn't say when that would be."

So Mattson was in the picture now. Quinn considered that fact a moment, realizing it put a different face on the whole situation. The three of them would be hard to take if they forted up somewhere. If they had enough time, there was a chance they could drum up some help from the Smoky Hills bunch, and Quinn and the whole

Flagg crew could be wiped out in an ambush.

Quinn glanced around the circle of faces, still sullen and tight-lipped, and it occurred to him that Ardis Kline could shoot as straight as Roland or Mattson, and fighting her wasn't going to appeal to his men. If it came to that, he wasn't sure he could even keep them in line.

"One more question, Monroe," Quinn said. "Which way did they go?"

Monroe jerked a thumb toward the ridge to the west. "That way. They was going up the trail the last I seen of 'em."

"They went that way, all right, boss," Pete Blackdog said. He had just ridden up. Now he jerked a thumb behind him toward the ridge. "Three of 'em. Didn't look like they've been gone very long. Mebbe less'n two, three hours."

"All right, Monroe," Quinn said. "You stay here. I may have use for you before the day's over. If you do what I tell you, you won't get hurt."

"I'll be here," Monroe said.

"Mount up," Quinn ordered, and, stepping into the saddle, started up the ridge.

The slant was not steep, for the trail followed the crest of the ridge that lifted slowly, but Quinn had pushed the horses too hard to keep the pace up. Presently he signaled a stop and motioned for Blackdog to get down and study the trail. He chafed at the delay, hating to lose even a minute.

The way he saw it, his one chance of catching Roland was to close the gap and get him before the three of them recruited help.

Blackdog rose. "They're still ahead of us, but we ain't far behind 'em."

"Then we'll keep on their tail," Quinn said.

"You trying to kill our horses and put us afoot?" Stub Moon asked.

Moon was a loud-mouth and Quinn had no intention of letting him get started. "We've got a job to do," Quinn said. "Let's do it."

He went on, Blackdog behind him, the rest strung out behind him. He didn't stop again until they reached the fork in the trail. Again he motioned for Blackdog to get down. He watched the cowboy walk slowly along the main trail, then come back and follow the north fork for twenty yards or more.

When he returned, Blackdog said: "Two of 'em stayed on top. One of 'em took the north trail."

"Where does it lead?" Quinn asked.

"Circles down off the ridge," Blackdog said, "then curls around till it comes to the river several miles below the Kline place."

"Got any notion which one went that way?" Quinn asked.

Blackdog shook his head. Quinn sat hunched forward in the saddle, his muscles aching with the tension that gripped him. They had separated to fool him, he knew, but he was a jump ahead of them. They were figuring he'd think Roland was heading for the state line and the girl was circling back to her place.

Well, he wasn't going to be fooled that easy. He saw through their trick. Roland was going back to the Bar C, so he was the one who had taken the north trail. When he reached the river, he'd swing upstream past the Kline place and follow the gorge to the mesa. The girl and Mattson were probably meeting some of the Smoky Hills men and were rigging an ambush along the trail. But Riley Quinn wasn't walking into their trap.

He hipped around in his saddle to face his men. "Looks like Roland has gone off on this north trail, but we can't be sure. Midge, you take Rance and Jones and follow the tracks on the ridge trail. If you find Roland, get him, but if you're following the girl and Mattson, let 'em alone and head back. The rest of you come with me."

He started down the north trail, watching the tracks ahead of him. He was fully aware that Roland might leave the trail and hide in a cedar thicket, hoping they'd go on by. Now he wished he'd waited for Slim Ives to get back from town. He could depend on Ives. He thought he could count on Midge, but he wasn't at all sure of Jones and Rance. At least he had the loud-mouth, Stub Moon, with him. If Moon started talking again, about horses or the girl or anything else, he'd shut him up good.

Suddenly Quinn realized he had lost Roland's tracks and reined up, cursing. "He took off back there somewhere, Pete," he said. "Pick up his trail for us."

Blackdog rode back up the trail a short distance, then called: "Here!"

"Lead out," Quinn said. "He ain't gonna make much speed through the cedars."

Blackdog hesitated, not liking it, but he obeyed. If they ran into Roland, he'd probably shoot the lead man, and that would be Pete Blackdog. But they'd have Roland, Quinn thought savagely. He could afford to lose his tracker if they got Roland.

For half an hour or more they followed Blackdog through the scrub oak and serviceberry brush, sometimes dropping down a steep, boulder-strewn slope, and finally reaching a small park with a spring breaking through the ground on the upper side. There, lying beside the spring, was Rusty Mattson, asleep.

Quinn had his gun out and was covering Mattson when the sound of their approach woke him. He sat up, blinking, and reached for his gun. He stopped, his hand in mid-air when Quinn said: "You touch that hogleg, mister, and you're dead."

Mattson rose, his hand dropping to his side. He asked: "What do you gents want?"

"Clay Roland," Quinn said. "Where is he?"

"I don't know," Mattson answered. "What do you want him for?"

"I'm asking the questions, not you," Quinn snapped. "You left the Kline place with Roland and the Kline girl. Where are they?"

Mattson was the same height as the Flagg foreman, but beside Quinn's great bulk he looked like a spindly-legged boy. He stood his ground, returning Quinn's stare. "You're off your stamping ground, Riley. You're supposed to stay on your side of the river if we stay on ours. Remember?"

Quinn took a step forward, so furious he was trembling. He had expected to find Roland instead of Mattson, and now he was angry at himself for making the wrong guess. It could easily be a fatal mistake. Now Roland had another hour's bulge at least, and Quinn had no hope that the three men he had sent on up the main trail would succeed in finding Roland. He would have been smarter if he had divided the crew equally, but it was too late now to think of what he should have done.

"Mattson, we ain't got time to fool with you," Quinn said. "Either you tell me what I want to know and do it *pronto*, or I'll kill you where you stand."

Mattson's leather-dark face turned bitter, his gaze swinging to the men behind Quinn, then back to Quinn. He had the look of a man who knew he was about to die and didn't really care, one way or the other. He said: "You shoot me down in cold blood, Quinn, and I'll haunt you as long as you live."

Behind Quinn, Stub Moon said: "Don't do it, Riley. Murder may be your style, but it ain't ours."

Quinn heard him, but he didn't turn or say anything to Moon. The hammer of his revolver was eared back, his finger tight on the trigger. "Mattson, I'll give you ten seconds. That's all the time you've got if you don't talk."

Mattson laughed in his face. "The brave Riley Quinn, shooting a man down in cold blood without giving him a chance for his gun. That's enough to blackball you in hell. You're just like the Flagg bitch you work for. . . ."

Quinn pulled the trigger. He saw the powder smoke drift downslope from him, he heard the roar of the shot, and felt the buck of the walnut handle against his palm, and he saw Mattson drop. He had the weird feeling that he was watching this scene but was apart from it, then he knew he wasn't and he lost all trace of self-control.

Panicky because he sensed he had just made the biggest mistake of his life, he pulled the trigger again and again until the gun was empty, every bullet slamming into the lifeless body of the man on the ground in front of him. He couldn't stop; he was a machine that had been wound up too tightly and had to run down.

The hammer dropped on an empty. He reloaded, then his right arm fell to his side. Suddenly he was limp and a little sick, and as he watched blood bubble from the dead man's mouth and run down his chin, he knew this was worse than a mistake. By one stupid, wanton act he had ruined everything.

He was not surprised when Stub Moon said: "Drop your iron, Riley. This is where we split up. We've taken a hell of a lot off of you, but we're done. We ain't riding for no outfit that murders a man like you just done."

Quinn whirled, thinking he had bulled through worse situations. He'd bull through this one. "Get down off that horse, Stub. I'm going to beat hell . . ."

He stopped, hard hit by the knowledge that he had never faced a situation like this. All the men had their guns in their hands and were pointing them at him. He had expected Moon to have his gun out, but not the others. His gaze moved along the line until it fastened on Pete Blackdog's swarthy face at the end. He dropped his gun, knowing it was no use. He had looked at plenty of men who hated him, but he had never before seen the complete revulsion that was in the faces of these men.

"Back up," Moon said. "Stand over there on the other side of the spring. You try to get that gun or make a move for your Winchester, and we'll come back and fill you fuller of lead than you filled Mattson."

Quinn obeyed. This was a nightmare, he thought. It had to be; it was an impossible thing that couldn't be happening.

Then Moon said: "I didn't think you'd do it, Riley. I'd have shot you in the back if I had." Moon's lips curled in contempt. "I reckon we're all wondering why we ever worked for you as long as we have."

Moon rode off through the brush, the rest following. A moment later they disappeared on the other side of a thicket of scrub oak. Quinn wiped his forehead. This had not been a nightmare. He was lucky to be alive.

He picked up his revolver and dropped it into his holster. He moved toward his horse in a daze, then the full impact of what he had done came to him. He couldn't go back to the ranch and tell Bess he had lost the crew; he couldn't go back and tell her he had failed to get Clay Roland.

He stood beside his horse, a hand on the horn. That was when the solution came to him. If he could flush Roland into the open and kill him, he would have accomplished what he started out to do. He could hire another crew. He had no chance alone against Roland, but if he could get him into town, he could find plenty of men to help him. Bill Land. Doc Spears. Ed Parker. Sure, he'd find enough.

The crew had ridden downslope and would take the north trail to the river. The ridge trail was the closest route back to Kline's, so he would go that way. He swung into the saddle and started climbing, satisfied with himself now that he knew exactly what to do.

Chapter Eighteen

As Clay rode up the cañon, leading Ardis's horse behind him, he wondered sourly why he had let her lead him into a box cañon like this. Sure, they could defend themselves in the stone cabin as long as their grub and water held out. The cabin had been built under an overhanging ledge so that the ledge formed part of the ceiling. Anyone standing on the rim above them could not see the cabin, so at least they wouldn't have to worry about an attack from that direction.

The trouble was Riley Quinn was a dogged kind of man. All he had to do was to sit down out there in the mouth of the bowl. It would become a question of who could hang and rattle the longest, but sooner or later Quinn, if he stayed, would starve them out. More than that, it would be easy enough to sneak past the cabin at night and steal the horses.

Looking ahead, he saw that he was riding into a cliff that was the dead end of the cañon. Apparently the stream flowed out of solid rock. But Ardis had said there was a corral up here where he could leave the horses. Maybe she had never been here before. She'd probably just heard about the place and was mistaken.

Another fifty feet showed him that Ardis knew

what she was talking about. The creek made a ninety-degree turn to the left, the cañon so narrow at this point that the sky was no more than a blue slit overhead. He had to keep his horse in the water. There simply wasn't any bank.

A moment later he discovered that the creek made another sharp turn, this time in the opposite direction. The cliff he had seen ahead of him was a long narrow point around which the creek flowed. Above it the cañon widened out into another bowl similar to the one below the stone cabin.

Here was plenty of grass for the horses. Unless Quinn or some of his men had been here before, or knew about the cañon, they wouldn't know this upper bowl was here, so the horses were probably safe enough.

Clay rode through a gate in a pole fence that had been built across the opening end of the bowl. He found it solid enough and slid the bars into place, closing the gate. He pulled off the bridle of Ardis's horse and stripped gear from his own, turning both animals loose.

For a moment he stood studying the sandstone cliff to the west. The creek boiled down the face of the cliff in a series of waterfalls. Beside each waterfall he saw toeholds that had been dug in the sandstone. Then he understood.

This was an outlaw hide-out known only to the fraternity and the Smoky Hills people. Close as it was to the Utah line and Robber's Roost, it was perfect for a man on the dodge. Even if he was tracked as far as the stone cabin, he could hold off a posse till dark, then slip out and escape by climbing the cliff. The members of the posse wouldn't know for hours that he was gone, and by that time the outlaw would probably have stolen a horse or bought one from a nearby rancher.

Clay walked back to the cabin carrying the bridles and his saddle and blanket. A strange world here in the Smoky Hills, he reflected, a world without law, an island unexplored by sheriffs and deputies. He doubted that Quinn or any of his men were familiar with this place. Probably he could stay here with Ardis as long as he wanted and be perfectly safe.

He picked up Ardis's saddle and blanket below the cabin, and climbed the steps, thinking he had never been as tired in his life. If he had his choice, he'd be here a long time.

He dropped the saddles and blankets inside the cabin and looked around. The interior was neat and clean, so the cabin had probably been used not long before. He saw two loopholes on each side of the door that let in some light, but there were no windows.

Someone had gone to a good deal of trouble to build this cabin and furnish it, he thought. He guessed that it had been the work of Long Sam Kline who had lived on the fringe of this outlaw world for a long time. He had probably sold them supplies and horses at a great profit to himself, and had guaranteed them a hide-out that would be far safer than the roadhouse on the river.

The door was a heavy, thick one that would stop almost any bullet. The cabin was furnished with a couple of rawhide-bottom chairs, a table, two bunks, and a small range. In the corner above the stove were two shelves filled with a variety of canned goods.

Amused, Ardis watched him from where she stood beside the stove. She asked: "Satisfied, Clay?"

"I sure am," he said. "I've done a lot of outlaw chasing, but I never ran into a place like this. I guess we could hold off the entire Flagg crew till we ran out of grub and water."

"They'd get tired before that," she said. "There's a seep off the cliff that never goes dry." She motioned toward the back side of the cabin. "It isn't enough water for an army, but there's plenty for the two of us. Besides the grub we brought, there's enough in those cans to last a long time. The only thing we don't have is wood, so after we eat you'd better fetch some in. There's an axe in the corner."

He sat down at the table. "This your dad's work?"

She turned to the stove to fork the bacon from the frying pan into tin plates. "That's right. I wouldn't have known about it if Pa hadn't built it. In fact, I didn't know about it for a long time, but he brought me up here last spring. He said we might find it handy sometime. He didn't do the rustling they accused him of, but he did take money from men on the dodge who were willing to pay high for a place to rest where they'd be safe. I'm not proud of him, Clay. He wasn't proud of himself, either. He aimed to sell out and leave the country this fall, but they didn't let him live long enough to do it."

"Why did they murder him? It seems more senseless than Dad's killing."

She shrugged. "How does anyone know what goes on in Bess Flagg's mind? I told you she was like a mad dog and should be killed like one."

"She may be a mad dog," Clay said, "but she's not crazy. She has a reason for everything she does."

"I guess so," Ardis admitted. "She probably believed the rustling talk. Or maybe she just didn't like anyone she couldn't run. She sure couldn't run Pa."

Ardis was silent while she brought the coffee pot to the table and filled the tin cups. Then she went on: "I think she's afraid of people she can't handle. It's safer to kill them and get them out of the way. It's probably the reason she's after you as hard as she is. The men who live in the hills are like Rusty and Monroe. They'd have done anything for Pa. Maybe Bess was afraid that someday he'd round up a bunch of his friends and raid her outfit. There's been a lot of that talk, too, you know."

Clay nodded. "I just thought of something else. We were going to stay on the trail. Keep ducking and running, but I guess you were a jump ahead of me. The hills boys know what I've been, so they won't be likely to help or hide a man who carried a star as long as I did."

"I was afraid to trust them," she said. "I thought this was a better bet."

"You're smarter'n I was on that," he said.

She gave him a searching look. "That's hard for you to admit, isn't it?" she asked. "You've lived by yourself so long you think you don't need other people's help. That's wrong, Clay. There are times when we all need help. I was in the best position to help you. Rusty and me, I mean."

She filled the tin plates at the stove and brought them to the table. As she sat down across from him, he said: "Yes, I guess it is hard for me to admit." He looked at her a moment before he began to eat, realizing only then how tired she was. "You'd better take a nap this afternoon."

"So had you," she said. "If they track us here, we'll probably be up all night."

"None of Quinn's men know about this cañon, do they?"

"I'm sure they don't," she said. "It's a well-kept secret. Of course a good tracker like Pete Blackdog could trail us here."

"I'll fetch the wood in," he said. "If they do find us, we'll bar the door and let them sweat." He grinned. "Trouble is you may get tired of my company."

"No, Clay," she said quickly. "Not ever." Then she lowered her head, her face flushing with embarrassment.

She had not intended to say that, he thought. They finished the meal in silence, Clay's mind turning back to the lonely years he had carried the star, and because he had been lonely, he had thought about Linda. It was natural that he would, Linda being the only girl he had ever loved, but he knew Rusty had been right about her. She'd led him around by the nose, all right. He'd been blind and that was a fact.

The strangest thing that had happened to him since he'd come back was finding in Ardis the characteristics he had mentally given Linda. He hadn't thought any woman would do what Ardis had, freely because she wanted to and without even being asked.

He glanced at her across the table, feeling a love for her that was overwhelming and completely unexpected, but he could not tell her. Not until he had won his fight. The odds were still too long against him. If he died, it would be better if she didn't know how he felt.

When he finished eating, he rose. "I'd better get at the wood chopping."

"What are you going to do, Clay? When we leave here, I mean?"

"I don't know," he said. "I haven't cut the odds down any, but sometimes a man gets help from unexpected places. I've seen it happen a lot of times. But I'll win. I've got more to fight for than Queen Bess and Riley Quinn and the rest of them put together."

He picked up the axe and went outside. He found a dead piñon not far from the cabin and worked for an hour or more, piling the wood at the base of the steps. He carried an armload inside, and, seeing that Ardis was asleep on one of the bunks, he eased the wood to the floor so he would not waken her. He moved to the bunk and stood over her for a moment, watching her breasts rise and fall evenly in her sleep.

The fire was out and the cabin was cold. Picking up her saddle blanket, he spread it over her, then he sprawled out full length on the other bunk and instantly fell asleep. It seemed only a moment later that Ardis was shaking him awake. He opened his eyes to look into her frightened face. He sat up, sensing what had happened before she said: "They're here, Clay."

Chapter Nineteen

Linda could not guess what motive had driven Bess to make the trip to town unless it was to see Bill Land and force the marriage. Bess had no real reason to force the marriage, Linda knew, except her hunger to control the lives of others, a hunger that had grown from the time of her accident into an obsession.

Now that Bess was gone, Linda wished she had told her straight out that she was giving Bill's ring back to him just as soon as she could, that she was marrying Abe Lavine and they were leaving the country. But it was a foolish thought. She wouldn't have the courage to tell Bess if she were here. She couldn't stand up to Bess, not on anything Bess felt as strongly about as she did this.

The more Linda thought about it, the more frightened she became. She wanted to see Lavine, to tell him they had waited too long now, that if he loved her, he would take her away today. Now! He would have taken her yesterday, but no, she'd had to play her feminine rôle and put him off. It was her own fault she was still here. The thought did not bring her any satisfaction.

Going upstairs, she packed everything she owned into a small trunk and two suitcases. She kept turning to the window to see if Lavine was in sight. She had to talk to him, but she didn't want to go to the bunkhouse. When, near noon, she did see him in the yard near the corral gate, Pete Reno was with him.

By noon the packing was finished. When she went downstairs, Ellie had her dinner on the table. She ate absent-mindedly, knowing that she couldn't wait any longer. She had to see Lavine soon, regardless of Pete Reno. She went upstairs to her room again, trying to think what she would do if Lavine changed his mind about her. She had saved some money. She'd go away somewhere, to Montrose or Grand Junction, or maybe Denver, and get a job. Something! Anything! She had to get away from here. If she stayed, Bess would find some way to make her marry Bill Land.

For a moment she thought of Clay Roland and immediately put him out of her mind. She would never love another man in quite the way she had loved Clay. Six years ago she could have had him. If she had been completely honest with him yesterday when he had kissed her and had broken her engagement with Bill Land then, she might still have had him. But now it was too late. To keep thinking of him was idle dreaming. She had lost him forever. Abe Lavine was her only chance and she must not lose him.

When she could stand it no longer, she carried

her suitcases downstairs and left the house. Lavine and Reno were squatting in front of the corral gate, whittling. They rose when they saw her coming, Reno's speculative gaze fixed on her from the moment she stepped off the porch until she reached them.

She always sensed something unclean about Pete Reno when he looked at her; it was in his eyes, in the expression on his pimply face. She shivered, a series of prickles running down her spine, but she succeeded in smiling at Lavine, refusing to speak to Reno or even look at him.

"I want to see you a minute, Abe," she said.

Lavine jerked his head at Reno. "Vamoose."

Affronted, Reno stared at him a moment, then turned on his heel and walked off. When he disappeared into the bunkhouse, Lavine said: "We're finished. If I don't kill him, he'll shoot me in the back."

"You mean because I came out here?"

Lavine shook his head. "It happened this morning. Quinn took the crew out to hunt for Roland. He threw it up to me 'n' Pete for not going. We're paid for fighting, he says, but we don't do nothing but sit around the bunkhouse all day while they go out and do what we're paid for.

"I told him I had my way of doing things and I wouldn't do 'em his way. Then Pete spoke up and said he'd go. When we hired on here, we agreed

195

I was to call the turn on everything. I told him he wasn't going. He got sore then and started to cuss me, so I slapped him. I thought he was going to draw on me, but he walked off. Well, it's been eating on him ever since."

"I'm sorry if I had anything to do with breaking you up," she said.

"You didn't." He smiled at the idea. "It's been coming a long time. Should have come sooner." He looked at her, his usual barren expression giving way to one of naked hunger. "Let's talk about something pleasant. You 'n' me, for instance."

"Take me away, Abe," she said. "I'll marry you any time you say. I knew yesterday that would be my answer. I don't know why I waited."

"I don't, either," he said, and, taking her into his arms, kissed her long and hard, not caring if Reno or the cook or Ellie saw them. Then he let her go and looked down at her, shaking his head a little as if not understanding how this had happened. "I never thought I could be this lucky."

"I'll be a good wife," she said. "I'll try as hard as I can, but right now you've got to get me away from here. I'm scared, Abe."

He pulled her close, holding her soft body against his. "I won't let anything happen to you. What are you scared of?"

"Bess. She's been good to me most of the time,

but it's all on the surface. She's bad. Even after living with her for two years, I didn't know how bad she was until she tried to kill Clay. Then this morning she said I had to marry Bill Land right away, maybe this afternoon. She'll do anything to make me do it. Anything."

"Go pack up," he said. "Won't take me long."

"I'm ready now. I've got two suitcases and a trunk inside. We can't carry them on a horse."

"Then we'll wait till she gets here and take the wagon. I can send it back from town. I've got some wages coming. I'd like to collect 'em before I go." He motioned toward the house. "You wait inside. I'll saddle up and be ready to go when she gets here."

She obeyed, thinking it was a mistake, that they should leave now regardless of her things or Lavine's wages, but she couldn't risk telling him. That was the way their married life would be. He was a strong-willed man whose decisions would not be changed by her or anyone. Even Bess had failed with him.

Linda waited impatiently, and finally she dragged her trunk down the stairs and left it beside the suitcases. After that she couldn't think of anything to do. A moment later she saw Lavine in front of the house with his horse and she sighed in relief. Maybe it would be all right to suggest they leave now. She could ride behind the saddle.

But she didn't make the suggestion, for when she stepped through the door to the porch, her coat and hat on, she saw Bess and Ives coming in the wagon. She walked to Lavine and stood beside him, her hand on his arm. He looked at her, frowning. He said: "We'll get married as soon as you give Land's ring back to him and we can find the preacher, but there's one thing I've got a right to know. Are you still in love with Roland?"

Her heart missed a beat, but she met his gaze, knowing this was one time when she had to be honest. "He was the first sweetheart I ever had. Can you understand that, Abe? There's a little spot in my heart that belongs to him, but I wouldn't marry him if I could."

Lavine nodded as if he did understand how it was with her. He was silent as Ives drove the wagon to the porch. Reno was striding toward them from the bunkhouse, but Lavine ignored him. Ives pulled up and, stepping to the ground, untied the wheelchair and lifted it to the ground. Linda, looking at Bess, wondered if she had a fever. Linda had never seen her cheeks so flushed.

Reno reached them, his gaze turning to Lavine for a moment, then to Bess. He said: "Missus Flagg, is Ives staying here or leaving to catch up with the crew?"

"He's leaving," she answered.

"I want to go with him," Reno said eagerly. "I wanted to go this morning, but Abe wouldn't let me."

"You don't take orders from Lavine if you work for me," Bess said. "You'll go with Ives."

"Thank you," Reno said, and ran toward the corral to get his horse.

Judging from the way Ives glowered at Bess, Linda thought he didn't want Reno with him, but he shrugged and walked away, leaving the wagon in front of the house. Bess laughed, an unpleasant sound that Linda had never heard her make before.

"Well, Lavine," Bess said, "you've been high and mighty with me for a long time, but I don't need you any more. I'm going into the house to get your money, but if you want it, you'll have to put the team away."

It was a calculated insult, the final bending of Lavine to her will, but, instead of obeying, he walked to her as he said: "Yes, ma'am, but first I'll roll you into the house."

She didn't protest, although Linda thought she seemed puzzled by this reaction. If Bess noticed that she had her hat and coat on, she ignored it. Linda followed them inside, then Lavine stepped back.

"Now that I think about it," he said softly, "the *dinero* ain't real important. Let's say I'll swap it to you for the use of your team and wagon. I need it to take Linda to town. I'll see it's brought back by evening."

The flush deepened in Bess's cheeks. Then she discovered the suitcases and trunk on the floor. She screamed: "Linda, what's got into you? Bill's bringing the preacher out this afternoon or tomorrow morning, and you're marrying him!"

"No, I'll never marry him," Linda said. "I'm leaving. I've stayed here as long as I can."

"I've paid you well," Bess cried. "What the hell is wrong with you?"

"I'm marrying Abe," Linda said. "Not Bill Land."

"Lavine?" Bess was so shocked that her mouth sprang open and she stared at Linda as if this was too crazy to be believed, then the flush spread over her face until it was scarlet. "By God, you're not doing anything of the kind."

Lavine had started toward the trunk and suitcases, then swung around so that he stood back of Bess's chair, but her attention was fixed so intently on Linda that she didn't notice where Lavine was. She snatched her pistol from the seat beside her. Linda cried out, knowing she should have foreseen this, that Bess was out of her mind and would kill her before she would permit anything to happen that was so contrary to her plans.

Bess did not see Lavine step up behind her until his arm slid over her shoulder. He grabbed the pistol and twisted it out of her hand. As he stepped back, he said: "I never killed a woman in my life, Missus Flagg, but I will kill you if I have to. We're leaving. Linda is going to do what she wants to. Can you understand that?"

Bess sat there, her face turning so dark it was more purple than red, but for a moment she said nothing. Lavine handed the pistol to Linda. "She doesn't understand anything she don't want to. Keep her covered. I'll take your things out to the wagon."

As Lavine went through the door with Linda's suitcases, Bess found her voice. She screamed: "Ellie! Ellie, fetch me the shotgun. I'll blow their damned heads off."

But if Ellie heard, she ignored it. Bess began screaming obscenities at Linda. Lavine returned for the trunk. He said: "Come on." Linda backed through the door, keeping the pistol aimed at Bess. Then she realized she had no need for the pistol. The torrent of words was cut off. Bess was leaning forward, one hand over her chest, her face contorted as if she found it hard to breathe.

Lavine helped Linda into the seat, then climbed up beside her and, taking the lines, spoke to the team. Lavine said gravely: "You're free now. I've watched you a lot of times when you were with her and it always seemed to me she had you hypnotized. You should have known what she was a long time before she tried to kill Roland."

"I guess I should have," she agreed.

She was silent for a time, knowing why she had given the appearance of being hypnotized. She had been afraid she would do something to lose her job. She had been selfish, she told herself, putting security above everything else, even to the extent of telling Bill Land she would marry him. She was doing the same with Abe Lavine, but it would be different with him. She would see to it that he never regretted his bargain.

Impulsively she slipped an arm through his. "I'm free of Bess, so I can marry you," she said. "And you're free of her, too. It was coming to the place where you would have had to do some things you didn't want to if you'd kept on working for her."

"I know," he said gravely. "I'm worse than you because I knew exactly what she was, but I liked the wages I was getting, so I stayed on."

"Abe, if Clay Roland isn't killed by Quinn and his men," Linda said, "and if he comes to town, there's no reason now to fight him, is there?"

He looked at her a long moment, his strong-featured face taking on the barren expression she had seen so many times. He asked harshly: "Is Clay Roland going to be between us all of our married lives?"

"No," she said, knowing that this, again, was a time when she must not lie to him. "It's like I told you. I was in love with him once. I would hate to know that my husband had killed him, and I would hate it worse if it went the other way and he killed you. I would like to leave here knowing you two were friends."

His face softened. "No reason we can't be. He's a good man."

They went on, her arm still through his. She felt quite satisfied with herself now. On occasion he could be as hard as tempered steel, and on those occasions she could not change him, but she could learn to live with him when he was like that. Then she smiled, her mind turning to the $10,000 he had in a Denver bank. It was a pleasant subject to think about.

Chapter Twenty

Ardis's words—"They're here."—sent Clay running to the nearest loophole. Three men sat their saddles near the center of the bowl, their eyes on the cabin as if uncertain whether they should come any closer or not. He knew the man in the middle, a cowhand named Midge who had worked for the Flagg outfit before Clay had left the country. The other two were strangers.

"Only three of them," Clay said. "Looks like Rusty did what he set out to do. He's pulled Quinn and most of his men off our trail."

Ardis stood, staring through the other loophole. She picked up her rifle from where it leaned against the wall. "He may be dead by now," she said bitterly. "If he is, I'm to blame."

"No, you're not," Clay said sharply. "Neither one of us could have changed his mind and you know it."

"I guess so," she said. "Sometimes he acted as if he wanted to die. Several times when he was staying at our place, he kept me up most of the night just talking. He hated Bill Land because he thought Land didn't believe in anything. He called Land a hypocrite for selling out to Bess Flagg. He never found a place or a job that satisfied him, so he just rode around like a tumbleweed. He said more than once that he wished he had your courage. He liked to say that dying wasn't so bad if he found something that was worth dying for."

Clay glanced at her. "What makes you think he's dead?"

She continued to stare through the loophole at the Flagg men, refusing to look at him. "I don't know. Just a feeling."

"Maybe you're wrong. You said he could play hide-and-seek with Quinn for a week."

"He could, but maybe he didn't want to." She let it drop, her face close to the loophole. After a moment's silence, she asked: "What's bothering them?"

The three men hadn't moved. Clay wasn't sure whether they were staring at the cabin or the upper end of the bowl. From their position the creek would appear to flow directly out of solid rock.

"I'm guessing they think we might be in here, but they're not real anxious to find out," Clay said. "They can't locate our horses, and the fire's out, so they don't see any smoke. I'd be wondering, too, if I was in their boots. They tracked us in here, but now it just don't add up right for them."

Ardis raised her rifle to slide it through the loophole. She said: "They're close enough to shoot."

"Not cold turkey," he said. "I'll give them something to shoot at."

He picked up his Winchester and, opening the door, stepped through it, ignoring Ardis's protests. He called: "You boys looking for me?"

One rider whirled his horse and, bending low in the saddle, headed for the entrance to the bowl on a dead run. Midge had his gun in his hand. Now he threw a quick shot at Clay. The bullet struck the wall above Clay's head and screamed as it ricocheted away into space. The third man reached for his gun and had it clear of leather just as Ardis cut loose. Her first shot knocked his hat off his head, her second smashed his left arm. That took the fight out of him. He wheeled his horse and took after the first man.

Midge got off his second shot just as Clay squeezed the trigger of his Winchester. Midge's bullet went *thwack* into the heavy door beside Clay. He didn't fire again. Clay's bullet had apparently struck him in the chest. He dropped his gun and bent forward over the saddle horn. Gripping the horn with one hand, he turned his horse and rode slowly down the creek. Clay expected him to fall off his horse, but he was still in the saddle, hanging tightly, when he disappeared through the lower end of the bowl.

When Clay stepped back into the cabin, Ardis had put her rifle down. She glared at him, her hands on her hips as she said: "Clay Roland, you're a fool. They'll fetch Quinn and he'll have us bottled up here."

He leaned his Winchester against the stone wall. "Maybe I am a fool," he admitted, "but those boys didn't want us very bad. If they'd been paid killers like Lavine and Reno, I'd have cut them all down, but they're working cowhands. They didn't want us real bad or they'd have operated different."

She looked at the floor, her quick flash of anger dying. "All right, I was wrong," she said. "I guess I was scared. I was thinking of what might happen if they killed us." Then she shook her head and walked to the stove. "No I wasn't. I just didn't see any sense of you going outside and making a target out of yourself."

"It was too far for a handgun," he said, "so I figured they didn't have much chance of hitting me. It's my guess we put them out of the fight. Midge is a dead duck. You busted the arm of one of them, so he won't do any more fighting for a while. The way the first one took off he won't stop till he gets to the mesa."

"Clay," she said tartly, "I admitted I was wrong. Start a fire. I'll cook supper."

He obeyed, then went outside and started in on the piñon again. Maybe what he had done did look foolish to Ardis, but he had never been able to shoot a man down without giving him a chance. If he had remained inside, the situation would have continued the way it was, a sort of siege that was not to Clay's liking. This way the three men were gone and Clay and Ardis were free to leave the cabin if they wanted to.

Midge wouldn't go far, but one of the others might bring Quinn and the rest of his men. If they had killed Rusty, he hoped they did come. He'd get every one of them, he told himself, every murdering son-of-a-bitch who worked for Bess Flagg.

Presently Ardis called him to supper. After they finished eating, he left the cabin and walked upstream through the narrows, telling Ardis he wanted to see if the horses were all right. Actually he wanted to get away by himself for a while. He could not get over Ardis's hunch that Rusty Mattson was dead.

When he returned, he carried the rest of the firewood into the cabin. He had reached a decision and he might just as well tell Ardis. It was time that he turned the tables and became the hunter instead of the hunted.

Ardis had lit a candle when Clay shut and barred the door. She asked: "Want a cup of coffee before we go to bed?"

"No," he answered. "Ardis, I've been doing some thinking. I can't stay here because I can't get Rusty out of my mind. If Quinn killed him, I'll kill Quinn. That's a promise."

"You're leaving now?" she asked incredulously.

"Not till morning. If one of the men I let get away does fetch Quinn, I'd just as soon be inside this cabin as anywhere else, but if he isn't here by morning, I don't think he'll come. Now there's one more thing. If he doesn't show up, you're not going with me. I don't want to leave you here, either."

"Don't worry about me. I'll find a safe place." She sighed. "You're such a fool, Clay. Sometimes I think you're like one of King Arthur's knights. They had a code they lived by, too."

"I never heard of them," he said. "All I know is that I've got a job to do if Rusty's dead. He was my friend, a better friend than I knew when we separated."

"But you can't change what has happened to him," she said. "Don't you understand that what he did was to save your life? And that it's what I've been trying to do, too?"

"I know." He thought of Anton Cryder who wanted him to ride into Painted Rock after dark so he would be safe, but he hadn't done it. Now he couldn't stay here, either. He added: "Ardis, staying alive is not the most important thing in the world."

"It is with the men I've known," she said. "Most of them, anyhow, the ones who rode in looking for a place to stay, the men Pa brought to this cabin. You're not like them. You never were. I guess that's why I . . ."

She stopped suddenly and turned away from him. He went to her and, taking her by the arms, swung her around to face him. "You were going to say that was why you loved me, wasn't it. Why don't you go ahead and say it?"

She shook her head, trying to smile, but not quite succeeding. "It would be wrong for me to say it, Clay."

"It wouldn't be wrong if I told you I loved you, would it?" he asked. "I've been wanting to tell you, but it seemed to me that it wasn't right to tell you. If I didn't make it, I didn't . . ."

"Oh, Clay, Clay," she whispered. "I've been wanting to hear you say it all this time. It would have been cruel for you to die without telling me."

He took her into his arms and, pulling her hard against him, kissed her. She gave her lips to him, kissing him hungrily and lingeringly. Linda or no other woman had ever kissed him like that. When at last she drew her head back, he knew how much he needed her, and that now he had far more reason to stay alive than the compulsion of mere animal survival.

"It would have been a mistake not to tell you," he said. "I didn't know . . ." He checked himself, thinking of the years she had waited for him and wondering why he hadn't known, and why Linda had been in his mind so much. "If you're not sleepy, I'd like to talk for a while."

He pulled a chair up to the stove and, dropping into it, pulled her down on his lap. He had not realized before how hungry he was for talk, how much he needed it. He told her about his plans for the Bar C, then about his father and why he had left the mesa, and finally about the six lonely years he had been gone.

Later, lying in his bunk with a saddle blanket over him, he found it hard to sleep. Old memories long dead had been brought to life when he had talked to Ardis, and now they ran through his mind one after the other, but he always returned to Bill Land who had been his friend, and Rusty Mattson who was still his friend, if he was alive. He finally dropped off to sleep, but near dawn Ardis woke him.

"I'm cold," she said. "I've been lying there with my teeth chattering."

"I'll get you warm," he said.

He moved over against the wall and she lay down beside him. He took her into his arms, holding her so that within a few minutes the warmth of his body stopped her shivering and she dropped off to sleep. Presently she stirred and whispered: "Don't go away again, Clay. Not ever." He did not say anything, and she was asleep a moment later.

There was still no sign of dawn creeping through the loopholes when a sound outside rang an alarm in him. He tensed, not sure whether it was the wind or a night animal scurrying along the ledge in front of the cabin, or a man slipping carefully toward the door. For an instant he couldn't remember where he had left his gun belt, then it came to him. It was on the table, but in the darkness it would take time to find it.

He put a hand over Ardis's mouth and shook her awake. "I think we've got visitors," he said. He slid off the bunk and felt his way across the room until he reached the table. A moment later his searching hand touched the belt. He drew the gun from the holster just as Ardis reached him.

"I heard something," she whispered. "They can't break the door down, can they?"

"No," he said.

A man called: "Ardis? Roland? You in there?"

"It's Monroe," Ardis said. "I'll light a candle. Let him in."

"Not yet," Clay said. "He may have Quinn's gun in his back. Light the candle, then get back into the corner."

"Ardis!" Monroe called again. "Roland, let me in." Clay stepped to the door. "What are you doing here, Monroe?"

"I've got a message from Quinn for you," Monroe answered. "Damn it, let me in. I'm tired and cold and hungry."

"You alone?" Clay asked.

"Sure I'm alone."

Ardis set the lit candle on the table and moved

212

back to stand between the bunks. Clay lifted the heavy bar and let it fall, then yanked the door open and hugged the wall beside it, his cocked gun in his hand. In the feeble light of the candle he saw that Monroe was alone as he had said.

Clay shut and barred the door the instant the man was inside. "Why didn't you holler instead of sneaking up this way? You scared us good if that was what you aimed to do."

"It wasn't," Monroe said, "but I figured it was the only thing to do. You couldn't have seen whether I was alone or not if I'd stayed on my horse and hollered. I had a notion you'd think it was a trick of Quinn's, using me to get the door open."

Clay walked to the stove and started a fire. He said: "Well, what's the message?"

"Quinn stopped this afternoon," Monroe said. "Funny thing, too. I was in the kitchen, getting something to eat, when a bunch of riders went by heading upstream toward the gorge. I didn't look at 'em real close, but it was the Flagg bunch. Just after they disappeared, Quinn showed up. He looked funny, like maybe he was scared, but I reckon I was mistaken. I guess nobody ever scared Riley Quinn. Anyhow, he told me he'd been in the barn and wanted to know if I'd seen his boys ride by. I said yes, but I hadn't paid any attention to 'em. He didn't say what he'd been doing in the barn, or why he waited while his crew rode by, and I sure didn't ask him.

"He said they'd caught Rusty Mattson and the crew was taking him to town. He said for me to find you and tell you that if you got to Painted Rock before sundown, they'd let Rusty go, but if you didn't, they'd kill him. He said this was a hell of a lot easier than hunting you down."

"Did he think Clay would do it?" Ardis demanded.

"He sure did," Monroe said. "Nothing else you can do, is there, Roland?"

"No," Clay said. "Cook some breakfast for us, Ardis. We'll pull out soon as it's daylight. You'll stay at your place with Monroe."

He held his hands out over the crackling fire, thinking this over. He had no illusions about his chances, but as Monroe said, there was nothing else he could do. At least he knew where to go.

"It's a trap, Clay," Ardis said. "The whole crew will be waiting for you. The town, too. Can't you see that?"

"Sure, I see it," Clay answered.

"You can't go," she said. "You don't even know they've got Rusty." She whirled to face Monroe. "You didn't see him, did you?"

"No, but like I said, I didn't look at 'em real close," Monroe said. "I didn't even know Quinn wasn't with 'em till he came in from the barn."

"There's something funny about that," Ardis

214

said, "Quinn not being with his crew. You can't go just to commit suicide."

"Maybe I won't be committing suicide," Clay said thoughtfully. "Could be this funny business gives me a chance, though I don't know what it is. Quinn sure thinks he's got it rigged, but I never figured him much on brains, so I'll take a chance."

"All right, Clay," Ardis said sadly as she turned to the stove. "I'll get your breakfast."

Looking at her, he knew she didn't understand, but then, he thought bleakly, maybe no woman would.

Chapter Twenty-One

Long-established habit woke Abe Lavine at the usual early hour. It took a moment to clear the cobwebs of sleep from his mind, to realize he was a married man and that he was in bed with his wife in a hotel room. He rubbed his eyes and yawned, and turned as gently as he could so he would not waken Linda.

He looked at her for a long time, her black hair contrasting sharply with the white pillow case. He smiled and shook his head, thinking for what must be the millionth time that he was a lucky man. He should have told her weeks ago how he felt, but maybe she wouldn't have left with him then. Perhaps it had taken the events of the last few days to shake her free from Bess Flagg's influence.

Well, she belonged to him now and he would never give her up. The stage left late in the afternoon to connect at Placerville with the night train to Montrose. They'd be on that stage. Once he had her away from here, she would forget about Clay Roland.

He slipped out of bed and went to the window. It would be a clear, fall day filled with the warmth of Indian summer. He stared down into the empty street, thinking they would get breakfast and then he'd buy her a wedding ring at Walters's Mercantile. They'd go to Denver and he'd see she had a good time for a few days. No need to make definite plans yet.

He put on his drawers and undershirt and, going to the bureau, poured water into the bowl and began to shave. He wished the stage left early this morning. The sooner he got her out of here, the better. He was troubled by something that had happened last night, troubled because he didn't understand it and he felt that somehow it would affect Linda and him.

They had gone to their room after having had supper in the hotel dining room, then he'd had the idea that this was an occasion that called for champagne. He'd gone down the stairs, but before he'd reached the bottom, he'd heard Riley Quinn's voice.

Lavine had paused, wondering why Quinn was here. Not wanting any unpleasantness on this, of all nights, he had slipped noiselessly on down the stairs to the hall that led into the lobby. Standing in the shadows so he wouldn't be seen, he'd had a quick look at the desk. Riley Quinn, Slim Ives, and Pete Reno were standing there, Quinn saying they were going to the Belle Union, but they were staying in town and they'd be back.

They'd left the hotel, but Lavine had remained where he was for a decent interval, then he'd gone upstairs and told Linda the Belle Union didn't have any champagne. They'd have to wait until they went to Denver to celebrate.

He still couldn't make any sense out of it. He had never known Riley Quinn to stay the night in town; he didn't know where the rest of the crew was or why the men weren't with Quinn. Maybe it didn't concern him, but then maybe it did, and he didn't want trouble today any more than he had last night.

He finished shaving, thinking about the past night and how Linda had told him she'd make him a good wife. She'd made the best kind of a start, he thought. It had been a night he wouldn't forget. As he was putting his shaving gear away, he glanced into the mirror and saw that Linda was sitting up in bed.

"Good morning, Missus Lavine," he said.

"Good morning to you, Mister Lavine," she said, "and will you tell me what you're doing up this time of the morning?"

"Why, I just woke up . . ."

"And I suppose you thought you were in the bunkhouse and you had to get up for breakfast," she said tartly. "Well, you're not. Now you come and get back into bed with me."

"More?" he asked.

"Yes, more."

He laughed aloud, the first time he could remember hearing his own laughter. Suddenly the barren loneliness of his past life was gone. In its place was a new and pleasant warmth, a strange feeling, but a good and welcome one. It was not too late to salvage something from his life.

"You know, honey," he said, and paused, wondering why he had called her that, then went on quickly, "I want a boy. I want a girl, too, but she'll be your responsibility. The boy will be mine and I'm going to teach him a lot of things, things that nobody ever taught me."

"You'd better start working on it," she said. "I can't do it by myself."

"It will be a pleasant duty," he said.

When Abe Lavine woke again, he was startled once he looked at his watch and saw that it was after 11:00. He turned over to find Linda awake and smiling at him.

"Satisfied?" he asked.

"Satisfied and hungry," she said.

"We missed breakfast," he told her. "We'll have to be satisfied with dinner."

Before they left the room, he buckled his gun belt around him. Linda pointed at the holstered gun. "Is that always going to be a part of you?"

"It will be as long as I'm in Painted Rock."

"And after we leave?"

"I don't know," he answered. "There are a lot of men who won't let me forget what I've been and what I've done. I may meet some of them again someday."

"I understand," she said, and, putting her hand on his arm, left the room with him.

They had finished eating when Pete Reno entered the dining room and walked directly to them. Lavine scooted his chair back from the table, his habitual barren expression coming to his face. Reno was the last man he wanted to see.

"So you got married, Abe." Reno gripped the back of an empty chair and bent forward as if he couldn't see Linda clearly. "Is she a woman? A real honest-to-god woman?"

He was drunk. Lavine had never let him drink during the two years they had been together. Whiskey and guns don't go together, he had told Reno repeatedly. This was Riley Quinn's work, Lavine thought, and wondered why.

"You're drunk, Pete," Lavine said. "Better go sleep it off before you get into trouble."

"I've been drinking a little, but I ain't drunk." Reno kept staring at Linda who had turned her head to look out of the window. "Riley, he set 'em up for me. Said I'd been missing a lot of fun." He bent closer toward Linda. "Abe, your wife fooled you. She used to be Clay Roland's girl. You know that?"

"Yes, I know." Lavine rose. "Let's go over to the store, Linda. It's time I was buying you a wedding present, a little round gold one. We'll see if Walters has one that fits."

"Now wait a minute," Reno said. "There's something I want to tell you. Clay Roland's gonna be in town today. He's coming in to get killed."

Linda's face whipped around. She stared at him, her eyes wide with terror, her lips parted. "How do you know?" she whispered.

"See?" Reno said triumphantly. "First time she's looked at me. All I had to do was to mention Clay Roland's name."

"How do you know, Pete?" Lavine asked.

"I'm gonna help kill him," Reno said. "That's how. I'm gonna be the bait. I'll be out in the street when he shows up. I'll tell him I'm gonna kill him, but he won't get no chance to plug me. I'll draw on him, all right, but Riley and Slim Ives, they'll be over yonder at the corner of the store and they'll drop him before he gets his gun out." Reno waggled a finger under his nose, his face turning ugly. "But they might miss, so Bill Land's gonna be waiting in his office and he'll plug Roland sure. He's a good shot, Land is."

"How do you know Roland will be in town today?"

"Riley says so. That's how. He gunned Rusty Mattson yesterday, then the crew got sore at Riley and rode out of the country. Quit, the whole kit 'n' caboodle of 'em. Riley says I'm gonna get a good job."

"Killing Rusty Mattson ain't got nothing to do

with Clay Roland coming to town," Lavine said. "They're running a sandy on you."

"No they ain't," Reno snapped. "Riley, he got word to Roland he had Mattson and that he'd kill him if Roland didn't show up." He waggled his finger under Lavine's nose again. "I ain't forgot you hit me yesterday. You didn't have no cause to do that, so I'm aiming to kill you just as soon as we take care of Roland. You got till then to git out of town."

"I'll sure do it," Lavine said. "You scare me."

"You'd better do it," Reno said, and, straightening, turned and left the dining room, walking with exaggerated dignity.

"Was he lying?" Linda asked.

"No, he wasn't lying," Lavine said. "Let's go upstairs. We'll let that wedding present go for a while."

She walked beside him, holding back the tears that threatened her. When they were in their room with the door closed, she turned to him and put her arms around him. "Abe, I wanted to get away from here before this happened."

"So did I," he said.

"Isn't there anything you can do for him?"

"Yes," he said angrily. "I can kill Pete, then go after Quinn and Ives. Is that what you want? You're asking me to save Roland and maybe get myself killed?"

She began to cry, her face pressed against

his shirt. "I've told you before and I'll tell you again," she said when she had control of herself. "I'll make you a good wife. You'll never regret that you married me, but can't you understand how I feel? If I was somewhere else when this happened, I'd be sorry about it, but I'd know I couldn't have helped him. Now maybe we can. If we just stand still and let them kill him, I'd always feel that we were partly responsible."

He pushed her away from him and went to the window. He stood staring into the street that was still empty, although now it was the middle of the day. So the word was out. Reno wasn't in sight, but Lavine saw Quinn and Ives sitting on the bench in front of Walters's Mercantile. This was the way Queen Bess would want it, a trap, but one that was sure-fire, and Riley Quinn and Slim Ives were the kind who would spring it.

Linda came to him. She didn't touch him. She just stood beside him and stared down into the street. Then she said: "Abe, it isn't fair. If they were giving him a chance, I wouldn't expect you to do anything. That's all I'm asking for him, a chance for his life."

He looked at her, wishing that Clay Roland was dead. He had considered killing Roland himself. If he could erase the memory of the love she'd had for Roland, he would have done it before now, but he knew that was the one sure way of losing her. She had given all of herself to him last night. No man could expect more. He had no right to complain, no right to criticize her.

"All right, Linda," he said. "I'll do something for him because it's what you want. That's the only reason."

She put her arms around his neck and, pulling his face down to hers, kissed him long and hard. "I love you, Abe. I was never really sure until now."

"Well, then," he said, "it will be worth it. Don't leave this room. If you do, I won't interfere."

"I'll stay here," she promised. "Whatever you do, don't take any risks."

"I'll think of a way," he said, and left the room.

He hurried down the stairs, wondering where Reno had gone. He strode past the bank and climbed the stairs of the drugstore to Bill Land's office. He put a hand on the knob of Land's door, turning it, pulling his gun, and, throwing the door open, went in fast. Land had been sitting in a chair beside the open window, a rifle across his lap. When he heard the door open, he jumped up, the Winchester in his hand.

"Put it down," Lavine said. "I'll kill you if you make a move to use it."

Slowly Land leaned the Winchester against the wall. "You married my girl. Now you come barreling in here holding a gun on me. Aren't you ever satisfied?"

"There's proper ways of killing a man," Lavine

said, "but your way ain't one of 'em. You're cowards, sneaking, belly-crawling cowards, you and Quinn and Ives."

"Who told you?"

"Reno."

Land cursed bitterly. "I told Riley he couldn't trust that fool kid." He paused, his eyes taking on a speculative glint. "If it's money you want, I'll give you a hundred dollars to get out of here and keep your mouth shut."

"No," Lavine said. "Sit down where you were. Don't touch the Winchester."

Someone was running up the stairs. Lavine put his back to the wall. The door opened and Doc Spears ran in, breathing hard. "She's dead, Bill!" Spears shouted. "She had a heart attack yesterday. She sent the cook in to get me and I went right out, but I couldn't save her. She died this morning."

"Who?"

"Queen Bess, you fool."

"Pull up that other chair, Doc," Lavine said. "Sit down beside Land in front of the window."

Spears whirled. He looked at Lavine's face, then at the gun, and obeyed the order without a word. Lavine said: "This makes it different, don't it, Land? She propped you up for a long time, but the prop's gone now. No reason to kill Roland, is there?"

"Nothing's changed," Land said bitterly. "You

225

think I've forgotten how he beat hell out of me the other day? He brought all this on when he came back. Now I'll see him dead. By God, I will."

"All right," Lavine said. "We'll wait."

He walked to Land's desk and sat down on it, his gun still in his hand. A moment later Spears said: "That wasn't such a long wait. Here he comes."

Chapter Twenty-Two

Clay lingered only briefly at the Bar C. He sat his saddle, staring at the pile of ashes that had been the house where he had lived most of his life, at the blackened, twisted bedsteads and the stoves. He had expected this, yet he had not been fully prepared for what he saw.

The thing didn't make sense. If Bess succeeded in taking over the Bar C, she would have use for the buildings. Why, then, had she burned the house? Did she have a feeling she wasn't going to whip him? Or was it a case of her wanting to destroy something that was a monument to her failure with John Roland?

Clay shook his head and rode away. He could build another house, a better house than the one Bess had burned. The windows and doors had not been fitted as tightly as they should have been, and on cold days when the wind was blowing, it had been impossible to keep the house warm.

The part that hurt was the loss of little things, the keepsakes that were worthless if judged by their value in money but were priceless to Clay because they belonged to his childhood and could not be replaced—his boyhood toys, his father's chessmen, and, yes, even the dishes in the cupboard that he had used as a baby. At least he still had the picture of his mother and his father's letter.

When the buildings of Painted Rock loomed directly ahead of him, he became sharply alert, putting the loss of his house out of his mind. This was the end, one way or the other. He was convinced of that. He would die, or Riley Quinn would die, and Quinn was Bess Flagg's strength, not Lavine or Reno or the Bill Land. If Quinn had caught and killed Rusty Mattson, Clay had all the more reason to kill him.

Clay reined up at the edge of town and looked along the street. He had no idea what Quinn planned, now that he had Clay where he wanted him. The Flagg foreman was not a fast man with a gun, and Clay doubted that he possessed any great amount of courage when it came to gunfighting, so he would certainly rig a trap that was geared to minimum risk for himself.

Clay could not see movement along the street, no sign of life except for a black-and-white dog dozing in the sun near the archway of the livery stable and half a dozen chickens dusting themselves near the boardwalk in front of the newspaper office. Not a single saddle horse was tied at the hitch poles, no rigs, no teams.

Casually Clay dismounted and led his horse off the street, leaving him beside the newspaper office where he would be safe from stray bullets, then he returned to the street and stood there as he drew his gun from his holster, checked it, and eased it back into the leather.

He had realized from the time Monroe had brought Quinn's message that there was a chance the Flagg crew would be hidden along the street and would riddle him with bullets without giving him a chance, but he didn't think Quinn would be that stupid. In reality his scheme might be murder, but it would likely have the appearance of a fair fight so Ed Parker could say the killing was justifiable homicide.

Apparently Painted Rock was a deserted town, and this puzzled Clay as much as anything. Somebody should be in the street by now, Lavine or Reno or Quinn himself. A full minute passed with no one making an appearance.

"Quinn!" Clay yelled. "You sent for me, Quinn. Are you too yellow to show up now that I'm here?"

A man came into the street from the other side of the Mercantile. He didn't walk as a man would under ordinary circumstances, but appeared to lurch as if he had been pushed. Or maybe he was drunk. For a moment Clay had trouble placing him, then he recognized him. It was Pete Reno.

"Come on!" Reno called. "I'm gonna kill you, Roland. Missus Flagg told you to get out of the country, but you didn't do it. Now it's too late."

Clay paced slowly toward him, thinking his words had been a little slurred. Maybe Reno had been drinking to give him courage. He stood with his legs spread, right hand splayed over the butt of his gun. He was little more than a kid. Clay realized this as the distance shortened between them.

Something was wrong. Six years of carrying a star had sharpened Clay's feelings about this kind of thing. Quinn wouldn't send a boy to do a man's job, not even if the boy had some claim to be a gunfighter. Clay's gaze swept one side of the street, then the other, but he did not see anyone. He raised his eyes to the windows of the second story of the hotel, the offices above Doc Spears's drugstore, then the windows of Anton Cryder's office over the Mercantile, but still he glimpsed nothing suspicious.

Clay stopped walking. He called: "I want Quinn! Get off the street, kid."

Insulted, Reno shouted: "I ain't a kid! I said I was gonna kill you. It's what Missus Flagg hired me for."

"Where's Rusty Mattson?"

"Dead, just like you're going to be. Keep walking, Roland. Are you scared of me? That why you stopped?"

So Ardis's hunch had been right. Clay guessed he had known all the time. He didn't answer Reno, but started walking again, sensing that if he dived for cover, he'd draw fire from whoever was waiting for him farther down the street.

Someone had to show soon. It would be two or three men, but not the whole outfit, he thought, or they would have opened up before now. Just ahead and to his left was a water trough that would offer some protection if he reached it. The sun pressed warmly against his back. For this moment the street was deceptively quiet and peaceful, a strange and inconsistent scene.

He was close to Reno now, so close that he could see the abject terror on the boy's face. Reno wasn't drunk enough to stand and fight. Clay said: "What makes you think you want to die for Missus Flagg?"

Reno caved then as Clay had been certain he would. He whirled and lunged toward the doorway of the Mercantile. A gun roared, and he stumbled and fell. Before he hit the ground, Quinn and another cowboy appeared around the corner of the store building, their guns talking.

Clay made his draw, right hand sweeping his gun from leather. He took the cowboy beside Quinn first, his bullet smashing into the man's chest and spinning him around and knocking him into the dust. Quinn was running toward Clay, heavily and awkwardly. He bellowed: "Shoot! Damn it, shoot!"

But no other shot came. Clay swung his gun to the big man. Quinn stopped, apparently realizing he was doing a foolish thing. He fired again, the bullet kicking up dust behind Clay and to his

231

right. Clay, standing still now, pulled the trigger a second time just as Quinn was bringing his gun down for another shot. He never got it off. Clay's bullet knocked him off his feet, but he kept his grip on his gun as he fell.

Clay walked toward him as Quinn, by sheer willpower, used all the massive strength that was left in his stubby body to lift himself to his knees. He raised his head to look at Clay as he struggled to bring his gun up to fire again. Blood bubbled from the corners of his mouth and dribbled down his chin. Then his strength ran out and he toppled forward on his face.

Standing over him, Clay looked down at this man who had been Bess Flagg's strength and most effective tool. He heard Quinn's muffled voice: "Bill Land was gonna cut you down. He didn't do it."

His hands, palm down in the dust, clenched into fists. He was dead. Clay raised his head to see Anton Cryder, running toward him. Other men appeared along the street now, Walters and Parker and several more.

Cryder was the first to reach him. He held out his hand. "You've done a job no one else could do. The truth is you're the only man who had enough guts to try."

Clay shook his hand, then shook hands with the others. A strange thing, he thought, as if only now he had ridden into town after being gone for

232

six years. They were welcoming him back, these men who had wanted nothing to do with him the day he had fought Bill Land.

"You holding me?" Clay asked Ed Parker.

"Of course not," the marshal said. "A clear case of justifiable homicide."

"Who shot the kid?"

No one answered for a moment. Doc Spears had run across the street and was kneeling beside Reno. He looked back over his shoulder to say: "He'll be all right. Just a flesh wound in his thigh."

Then Walters said, slowly as if reluctant to tell how it had been: "Quinn shot him. He was bullet bait. He was supposed to pull you on, and they were fixing to smoke you down from the side. It would have given them an excuse, you see, Reno being Quinn's man."

"It wasn't quite that way," Lavine said.

Clay hadn't seen him come up. He wheeled, hand sweeping gun from leather again, then he froze, the gun in mid-air. Lavine was bringing Bill Land across the street, the muzzle of his gun prodding the lawyer in the back.

"Which side are you on now?" Clay asked as he holstered his gun.

"The right side, I'd say," Lavine answered. "Reno told me what they were fixing to do, so I dropped in on your old friend here. He was sitting at the window with his Winchester all loaded and ready for you. I got it out of him just before Reno made his move. Quinn and Ives weren't supposed to show at all. Land was going to fire the same instant Reno did. They were gambling Reno would get off one shot. Nobody, including the law"—he paused to look contemptuously at Parker, then continued—"would figure out that the bullet had hit you at a downward angle. It would have been justifiable homicide."

Parker, red-faced, said nothing.

"They fooled Reno into believing they wouldn't let him get killed," Lavine went on. "They said they'd get you before you fired a shot."

"Rusty's dead?"

Lavine nodded. "Quinn killed him yesterday."

Clay turned and walked off, sick because he could not save Rusty Mattson's life. He was sick, too, of the cowardice of these Painted Rock men who considered him a hero, now that Riley Quinn was dead. In a way he was surprised, for in time Queen Bess could hire another to take Riley Quinn's place and the whole thing would have to be done over again.

"Clay, we heard your house was burned!" Cryder called. "What are you going to do?"

"Rebuild it," Clay said. "It's my home. I'm going to live there and Queen Bess isn't going to run me off."

"That's right," Doc Spears said. "She's dead. She had a heart attack."

So that was it, Clay thought, the reason these men had found their courage. Again he started to turn. Lavine said: "What about your old friend, Roland? He was sure aiming to smoke you down. I think he ought to get down into the dirt and crawl out of town."

"I don't care whether he crawls, rides, or walks," Clay said, "but he better be damned sure he's out of town before I come back."

"I think he will," Lavine said. "I think he will." He holstered his gun, and, catching up with Clay, strode along beside him. He said: "Roland, there's something I've got to know. Would you marry Linda if you could?"

Clay looked at him sharply. "What business of yours is that?"

"A hell of a lot. Would you?"

"No. I'm going to marry Ardis Kline."

"Why now," Lavine said, pleased, "I'm glad to hear that. She sells a poor grade of whiskey, but she's a good cook." He held out his hand. "Would you shake hands with me, Roland? Linda's watching from our hotel room. You see, we were married last night and we're pulling out on today's stage. She said she'd like to leave here knowing you 'n' me were friends."

Clay hesitated, shocked momentarily by Lavine's statement that he and Linda were married. Then he gripped Lavine's hand. "Congratulations. Make her happy, mister, or I'll look you up."

Lavine laughed aloud, the second time that day. "I aim to try, Roland. I sure do."

Clay went on to his horse, Lavine turning back. Clay mounted, and, when he was in the street, he raised his hand in a sweeping salute toward the hotel. He wondered if Linda had anything to do with Lavine's interfering in a fight that was none of his affair. It wasn't like a man of Lavine's caliber. But he would probably never see Linda or Lavine again, so he would never know.

Turning his horse, Clay rode west across the mesa. Ardis would be waiting for him.

About the Author

Wayne D. Overholser won three Spur Awards from the Western Writers of America and has a long list of fine Western titles to his credit. He was born in Pomeroy, Washington, and attended the University of Montana, University of Oregon, and the University of Southern California before becoming a public schoolteacher and principal in various Oregon communities. He began writing for Western pulp magazines in 1936 and within a couple of years was a regular contributor to Street & Smith's *Western Story Magazine* and Fiction House's *Lariat Story Magazine*. *Buckaroo's Code* (1947) was his first Western novel and remains one of his best. In the 1950s and 1960s, having retired from academic work to concentrate on writing, he would publish as many as four books a year under his own name or a pseudonym, most prominently as Joseph Wayne. *The Violent Land* (1954), *The Lone Deputy* (1957), *The Bitter Night* (1961), and *Riders of the Sundowns* (1997) are among the finest of the Overholser titles. *Bunch Grass* (1955) and *Land of Promises* (1962) are among the best Joseph Wayne titles, and *Law Man* (1953) is a most rewarding novel under the Lee Leighton pseudonym. Overholser's Western novels, whatever the byline, are based on a solid knowledge of the history and customs of the 19th-Century West, particularly when set in his two favorite Western states, Oregon and Colorado. Many of his novels are first-person narratives, a technique that tends to bring an added dimension of vividness to the frontier experiences of his narrators and frequently, as in *Cast a Long Shadow* (1957) filmed as *Cast A Long Shadow* (United Artists, 1959), the female characters one encounters are among the most memorable. He wrote his numerous novels with a consistent skill and an uncommon sensitivity to the depths of human character. Almost invariably, his stories weave a spell of their own with their scenes and images of social and economic forces often in conflict and the diverse ways of life and personalities that made the American Western frontier so unique a time and place in human history.

Books are produced in the United States using U.S.-based materials

Books are printed using a revolutionary new process called THINKtech™ that lowers energy usage by 70% and increases overall quality

Books are durable and flexible because of Smyth-sewing

Paper is sourced using environmentally responsible foresting methods and the paper is acid-free

Center Point Large Print
600 Brooks Road / PO Box 1
Thorndike, ME 04986-0001 USA

(207) 568-3717

US & Canada:
1 800 929-9108
www.centerpointlargeprint.com